# WAR ON THE PORCH

A DOUGHBOY'S INTERVIEW

TWENTIETH CENTURY WAR STORIES
BOOK TWO

TRAVIS DAVIS

# AUTHOR'S NOTE

Some of the incidents and characters in this book are based on historical events and real people.

* * *

All times in War on the Porch for the battle scenes are in military time. For example: 1930 = 7:30 P.M. 1400 = 2:00 P.M. and 0200 = 2:00 A.M.

* * *

War on the Porch discusses Post Traumatic Stress Syndrome. If you're in crisis, please reach out to a medical professional, Veterans Administration, Clergy, or a Friend or Family member. You are not alone.

# TWENTIETH CENTURY WAR STORIES

TRAVIS DAVIS

***F.X. Regan - Best Selling Author of the CJ Hawk - FBI and Detective Kiki Diaz Thriller Series***

*Just like Travis's last book, "One of Four," his latest WW I saga, "War on the Porch," belongs in every junior and senior high school in the country. As the grandson of a WWI vet, I'm proud to see someone with Travis Davis' knowledge of The Great War keep history alive for future generations through his historical fiction. Bravo!*

# DEDICATION

*This book is dedicated to Thomas "Tommy" Miller, a young American soldier, a farm boy from Kansas. While he was in the trenches during a brutal German artillery barrage in World War I, the deafening roar tore through his senses as shrapnel rained down around him. When the smoke cleared, Tommy was left in the cold silence of blindness, his eyes permanently damaged by the explosion, his once-vibrant world reduced to a chilling darkness. While in a rehabilitation hospital in England, with a dedicated team of healthcare providers and a team of specialists, he learned to cope, navigate, and live with his blindness. Through sound, touch, and smell, he slowly rebuilds his sense of independence.*

*While in rehabilitation, he discovered a hidden musical talent, as his fingers danced across the piano keys; the melodies became a way to express the emotions he could no longer fully articulate. Using his newfound talent, he dedicated his life to advocating for other blind veterans. Sharing his experiences with fellow soldiers, he helped establish support networks for those who had lost their sight in the war. He eventually found a fulfilling role as a teacher at a school for the blind. He drew on his experience and leadership gained in the trenches of World War I, as well as his rehabilitation efforts in England, to inspire a new generation of students to embrace their potential despite their disabilities.*

*Tommy's story is a testament to the resilience of the U.S soldier blinded in the harsh environment of combat of World War I. He turned his disability into a gift that helped his fellow soldiers pursue their dreams and become the fathers of the Greatest Generation.*

* * *

*The 3rd Infantry Division held its ground during the Second Battle of the Marne in July 1918. With the bravery of the officers and men during that battle, they are now called "The Rock of the Marne." Since then, the division has participated in World War II, the Korean War, the Cold War, the Gulf War (also known as Desert Storm), the War on Terror, and the Iraq War.*

* * *

*Every one of the over 4 million Americans who supported the war effort both at home and abroad.*

* * *

*Especially the Doughboys.*

# ACKNOWLEDGMENTS

I would like to thank everyone for the love and support they provided me while I researched, wrote, rewrote, and edited War on the Porch.

Most of all, my wife, Martina, sat countless hours alone while I typed and researched the book.

Sabin Howard, for his support and friendship. The amazing sculptor of the World War I Memorial in Washington, D.C. His sculpture brings the war to life, allowing my imagination to run wild—an inspiration for the book.

*Sabin Howard - Working on one of the figures of the World War I Memorial (A Soldier's Journey) Sabin Howard*

*World War I Memorial at Pershing Park, Washington, D.C. 2024*
*The sculpture Soldier's Journey. Sabin Howard*

Thank you, Jeff Lowdermilk, for providing me with the necessary information regarding trench watches. He shared his grandfather's trench watch with me. Jeff's book, Honoring the Doughboys: Following My Grandfather's WWI Diary, is a fantastic book. I highly recommend it.

Last but not least, CAPT Chris Christopher, USN (Ret.) from the Doughboy Foundation. For his support and for connecting me with Jeff.

# PREFACE

With the advent of modern warfare, the worldwide human cost of World War I was a staggering 40 million plus casualties, of whom between 15 and 22 million individuals were killed. In just eighteen months of war, the United States suffered over 320,000 casualties, including 116,516 deaths and 204,000 injuries. Many soldiers returned home with visible injuries; some were missing arms or legs, while others endured severe head trauma. Some wounds were less obvious, such as blisters from mustard gas hidden by clothes, soldiers blinded by chlorine gas, and a condition known as "shell shock." Today, "shell shock" is understood as post-traumatic stress disorder. Many veterans came home with a combination of visible and invisible injuries. The American public was unprepared for the consequences of modern warfare and the effects that awaited them when soldiers returned home. The available resources, hospitals, and rehabilitation centers were insufficient to support the returning heroes. Many soldiers came from very rural areas of America, with very little infrastructure to care for them as they returned.

The Veterans Administration was established on July 21, 1930, twelve years after the war's conclusion. Prior to that, a limited number of military hospitals, community organizations, volunteers, and church groups were responsible for helping veterans transition back to civilian life, as many were eager to return to their pre-war lifestyles.

During those eighteen months of the war, their fathers, sons, and uncles returned home after facing the worst conditions imaginable: filthy, muddy trenches, gas attacks, machine gun fire, accurate long-range artillery, ten-round magazine-fed rifles, and death from above with the introduction of airplanes. There was no place on the battle-field to hide from death.

This is the story of a soldier who became blind as a result of an artillery attack. He overcame his disability, became an advocate for blinded soldiers, and established support groups for them. This is his story told in his own words.

# World War I Western Front
# Summer/Fall 1918

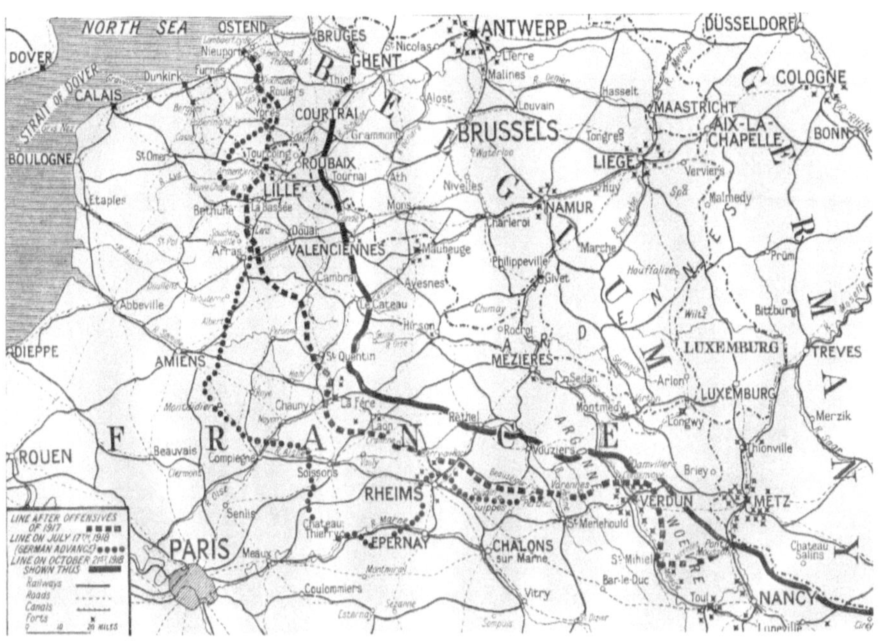

# CHAPTER 1



## LIFE CHANGING

It was early morning on what promised to be a sunny, hot, and humid July day in central Arkansas in 1968 as I drove with my windows down in my blue 1963 Chevy Malibu. I was heading to interview a World War I veteran. Earlier that summer, I had been assigned to write a feature article for the upcoming 50th anniversary of the end of World War I. At that time, I was a reporter for the Arkansas Gazette and had received the names of several World War I veterans living in Arkansas. One of them was a veteran who had overcome his disability but had never agreed to be interviewed, despite multiple requests over the years since the war's end. So, instead of contacting him beforehand, I decided to take my chances and drive to his house. I was very excited to meet him.

I grabbed my map from the passenger seat to see which exit to take. It took me only a minute to find my exit and put the map back on the seat. I hoped I wouldn't need it again. I took the Bald Knob exit 55 off Highway 67, turned onto 367, and then turned left onto South Elm Street, stopping at a small grocery store called "Buds Grocery" on the right. I grabbed my piece of paper with the address and went in. A young man was standing behind the counter.

I handed him the piece of paper, and he said, "Hmm, the King's house. It's the house before the turn on your left, next to the big tree." I thanked him, got back in my car, and drove to the location the clerk had specified.

As I got closer, I reconsidered my decision to drop in, but I was already committed. A quarter mile from the grocery store, at the turn in the road, I saw his mailbox, which read Mr. and Mrs. Patrick King. I had arrived at the right place. I stopped in front of the house and noticed an older gentleman sitting on the front porch, seemingly enjoying the morning sun. The weather over the past week had been miserable, with rain, thunderstorms, and sporadic tornadoes— almost like springtime weather. It seemed he decided to take advantage of the first nice day after a week of gloom. Looking at him, I wished I were doing the same, but I was under a deadline and had work to do. What I learned later from him was that he had always felt exposed and seldom sat outside. He told me later that he realized, as he grew older, that he needed to confront his fears and lay those demons to rest. I, too, had my demons, but I was not ready to engage them.

I pulled into the short driveway next to the house, and as I parked, I heard a dog start to bark. By the sound of the bark, it was a big dog. I almost didn't get out of my car, but I had gone too far to stop now. I opened my door and got out carefully so as not to injure my back again while shutting the car door. I walked toward the porch.

As I got closer, I heard, in a raspy voice, "Sarge, stop barking. Pauline, Honey, someone's just pulled up. Can you come out to see who it is?"

From inside the house, I heard, "Patrick, I can't. I'm taking my apple pie out of the oven. Just wait till they come up on the porch."

I was no more than ten feet from the porch when the dog's barking turned into a growl. I froze in my tracks. There, sitting in a rocking chair, was the veteran I had been searching for. I assumed he was sitting there feeling the warm sun on his face, basking in the light of a beautiful midsummer morning. Next to him was a stunning German Shepherd.

Standing up from his chair, he yelled from the porch, "Stop right where you are. Who is it? Can I help you?"

Standing before me was a person who was about to change my life, but I didn't know it at the time. It wasn't his outward appearance. He was unassuming, standing at 5'8" and weighing around 165, with balding gray hair and dark slacks, a white long-sleeved shirt with the sleeves rolled up halfway up his arms, a gray fedora with a black hat band, and black rimmed sunglasses.

I replied, "Hello, Sir, are you Patrick King?"

"Yes. Who wants to know?"

"Mr. King, I'm Gordon Grover, a reporter for the Arkansas Gazette.

"Great. I don't need a subscription. I don't read a lot these days."

"Sir, I'm not here to sell you a subscription," I said.

Before I could explain my reason for the visit, he responded, "Then why are you here?"

"Well, sir, with the 50th anniversary of the end of World War I approaching, I'm interviewing Arkansans who served in the war, and your name was mentioned. He sat back down in his chair, leaned back, and replied, "I'm not interested."

"Sir, it will only take a few minutes. I only have a few questions, please."

Waving his hand, he raised his voice and said, "No, please leave now."

I could see his wife standing behind the screen door, listening to every word of the conversation. Just as I turned to leave, she opened the door and said, "Young man, hold on. Don't leave so quickly."

Out walked Pauline King, standing 5'6", short gray hair, glasses, and a broad smile, a very beautiful woman, but I could tell she could be very forceful and determined.

"Patrick, you might want to be a bit more polite. He drove all the way from Little Rock to talk to you," Pauline said, her tone tinged with frustration.

Grumbling to himself, he muttered, "Damn it."

"I heard that, Patrick Wayne King." She continued, "Mr. Grover, please come up here and take a seat—right here, next to Patrick." She pointed to the chair beside Patrick.

She walked back into the house and said, "Make yourself at home. I will be right back."

I walked up the steps and sat down next to Patrick. I placed my briefcase on the ground and said, "Sir, I apologize for imposing, and I assure you it will only take a few minutes."

"Why didn't you call? We have a phone!"

"Well, sir, I understand that you have been contacted for interviews, but you have not yet agreed to one. Therefore, I decided, perhaps not my best decision, to drive out here and try my luck."

As I sat there, his dog approached me with its tail up, its curved tip, and started sniffing me. *I asked myself, Am I about to get bitten?* But based on what I have been told, if a dog approaches you with its tail up and its tip curled, it is pretty safe to pet it.

"What is his name, and may I pet him?"

"His name is Sarge, and yes, he loves it," replied Patrick.

I asked, "Sarge? That's an odd name for a dog. I don't think I've ever heard of a dog named Sarge."

"It's a long story," replied Patrick.

Pauline walked out of the house with a pot of fresh coffee. "Mr. Grover, would you like a cup of coffee?"

"Honey, he won't be here for long."

"Patrick, let him be. Stop being a grumpy old man. Mr. Grover, would you like a cup?"

I replied, "Yes, I would love one. Thank you, and please call me Gordon."

She poured me a cup of coffee and one for Patrick. Wow, it smelled amazing. "Cream or sugar, Gordon?"

When she asked, I already had the cup to my lips. I looked up over the cup, pulled it back, and said, "No, thank you. Pauline, this is the best coffee I have had in a long time."

"Come on, let's get to it. How many questions do you have, Mr. Grover?" Patrick asked.

"Sir, please call me Gordon. I have ten or so questions."

"Mr. Grover, you have thirty minutes," he replied, tension clear in his voice.

From what I was told by people who knew him, he hadn't said much about the war since returning in the spring of 1919. At best, when asked, he would answer questions about how he lost his sight. His typical reply was, "I went blind in the Great War after a German artillery attack." He never provided details, yet for some reason, I knew there was so much more to his story. Still, he kept it to himself.

Placing the cups on the table between the chairs, Pauline sat down across from her husband and said, "Son, take as much time as you need. He is not going anywhere." She could see on her husband's face that he was not too happy.

Little did I know at the time, but my conversation with Patrick would have a profound impact on my life. I would never be the same man again, and that would be a positive change.

# CHAPTER 2



FROM THE BEGINNING

I took my notebook and tape recorder from my briefcase and retrieved a pen from my front pocket. Patrick sat waiting for questions. His hands were clasped on his chest as if guarding something or praying.

Pauline rested her hand on his shoulder and gave it a gentle squeeze, offering reassurance. She understood that this would be challenging for him. Pauline confided in me after the interview that she only knew fragments, not the complete story, and she felt that he was hiding something.

"Sir, are you ready?" I asked.

Agitated, he replied, "Yes, yes. I'm ready. I want to get this over."

"Why did you join the Army knowing you were going to France and fight?"

"Let me answer all your questions now so you can leave. I didn't enlist. I was drafted in 1917. I had wanted to join earlier, but my parents thought I was too young to go off and fight, and they were against the war. So, I stayed home to help on the farm. I received my draft notice in late summer 1917. I reported to the Selective Board, passed my physical, and then went to Camp Greene in North Carolina for basic training. I was sent to France in the spring of 1918, specifically May, with the 3rd Infantry Division. I lost my sight on July 11th, which was right before the Germans launched their offensive, the Second Battle of the Marne, from July 15th to 18th. After spending a few days in a hospital in Paris, I was transferred to England for rehabilitation. I want to say that the people in England were great. There was one young nurse, I'm assuming, by her gentle and soothing voice. Her name was…"

Patrick tapped his right temple and said, "Lillie….. Marlene, that was her name, Lillie Marlene. Wow, I haven't thought about her for 50 years. She is the one who took care of me and many other soldiers. Once rehabilitation was complete, I was sent back to the States on a large ship. Upon arriving in New Jersey, I took a train to Little Rock to finish my out-processing and get some new clothes, where I received my demobilization allowance. Let me tell you, it was meager, to say the least. But it did help. Well, that's about it. Do you have any other questions?"

I wrote down his reply, looked up, and asked, "Were you and your beautiful wife together then?"

He began to rise when his wife said, "Patrick, stop being so ugly to him. He is only doing his job. Please sit down and allow him to ask his questions."

"Mrs. King, that's alright. I can see he doesn't want to talk about it. I felt similarly after World War II. It took me years to even mention it. All I wanted was to go home, finish my education, get married, and start a family."

Patrick sat back down, took a deep breath, and asked, "So, you were in the war? What did you do?"

"Sir,…."

He interrupted, "Gordon, please call me Patrick. I'm sorry. I owe you an apology. I spent my entire life helping soldiers. Look how I'm treating you."

"Sir, I mean Patrick. I was a pilot. I flew P-38s in Europe. My unit was the 474th Fighter Group, which was part of the Ninth Air Force.

And by the way, you couldn't have known, and I'm not offended. Honestly, look at what's happening now and how people are treating our soldiers returning from Vietnam. It's disgraceful. Now that truly offends me!"

I thought to myself that *my son might have to go to Vietnam. He registered for the draft just over a year ago.*

Patrick extended his hand to me, and we shook hands. I noticed a large scar on his right hand. Pauline took his other hand and squeezed. A smile began to spread across his face as he said, "Pauline and I met at a church dance in the spring of 1917. I had seen Pauline at church before, but I knew she was too good for me. However, that night at the dance, her beauty radiated. Her long brown hair flowed over her shoulders like a waterfall of chocolate milk."

"Chocolate milk, Patrick," Pauline responded, snickering.

"Hey, this is my story. She stood up to walk toward the punch bowl. I thought this was my chance to meet her, so I got up, tripped on my shoelace, and fell to my knees on the floor. I looked up, and there she was, her arms outstretched.

When I saw her brown eyes, they put me in a trance. I couldn't say a word. To say the least, I felt embarrassed."

He took a deep breath. The expression on his face conveyed everything he was feeling.

Then he continued, "I grabbed her hands, stood up, and was inches away from her. Before I could say a word, she remarked, 'I hope you dance better than you walk.' Since that night, we have been together almost every day—well, except for the time I was in the Army."

Pauline stood up, leaned over, and embraced Patrick, kissing his cheek and whispering, "I love you, clumsy."

He continued, "Initially, we kept it to ourselves. After all, I was the son of a dirt-poor sharecropper. While my dad was born and raised here, my mother was an Irish immigrant. I was a farm boy, and her dad worked at the local bank. I think he was the manager, right, Pauline?"

She nodded.

"You could say I was on the other side of the tracks. Heck, my parents didn't even have a bathroom in the house. We had an outhouse. Yet, I knew back then that I wanted to spend the rest of my life with her. Still, in the back of my mind, I realized I was going to be drafted. If not drafted, I'd enlist. The war against the Germans wasn't going well, and I had to do my part. My mother had immigrated to the U.S. from Ireland. My father was too old to serve, so I wanted to give back to a country that had given my family a new life. I wanted to give back to this country. I had to. I suppose you could say I felt a strong sense of obligation to serve my country. Back then, we were proud and loved our country."

Laughing, he said, "Now, getting back to Pauline, I tried not to get too attached to her, but the heart knows what the heart wants."

He took another deep breath and continued, "After the Fourth of July in 1917, Pauline came to visit. By that time, everyone knew we were courting. It seemed that her mother and father didn't mind, so we didn't hide our affection for each other. We were sitting outside near a fire, trying to keep the mosquitoes away. We were burning leaves, hoping the smoke would keep them away. But it was hot, as it always is that time of year, and the mosquitoes were out in full force. As we chatted, the mailman approached and said, 'Patrick, I have a letter for you.' He didn't mention who it was from. I figured he didn't want to upset Pauline, but I could tell as soon as I looked at it. It was a draft notice."

Patrick stopped and reached for his coffee, his hands trembling. He took a long sip and turned to his wife. She inquired, "Patrick, are you okay? Here, let me get you some more coffee or something else to drink?"

"I'm good. Some of these details I haven't thought about in years, but they're fresh in my mind. It feels like they happened yesterday. Pauline, you were so beautiful, and I know you're still just as beautiful." He removed his sunglasses, covered his eyes, wiped away his tears, and then put them back on.

"Patrick, do you want to take a break?" I asked.

"No, I think we are almost done anyway," he replied. Leaning forward in his chair, he said, "Let me backtrack. Earlier in the year, I turned twenty-one and had to register with the local Selective Service Board for the draft. At that time, I was given a serial number and a classification. There are five classifications, numbered 1 through 5. I was classified as a 1, which meant I was immediately liable for service. Classifications were based on age, family status, and occupation. Some jobs were deferred, like working in an ammunition plant. I think jobs contributed to the war effort, and if you worked at one of those, you were deferred.

After that, I waited for my notice to schedule my physical, assuming that the serial number I was given based on my birthdate had been drawn in a lottery. As fate would have it, my number was drawn in the first lottery, which took place on June 5, 1917. On that late-summer day when Pauline was here, I received my letter. I was ordered to report to the local Selective Service Board, located in Searcy, no later than August 20, 1917, for my pre-induction physical examination. At the time, we lived a few miles outside of town, so I would have had to walk to the bus station to take the bus to Searcy. I was lucky Pauline's father drove us all to Searcy in his Model T. Pauline, do you remember that old thing?"

"Oh yes, Patrick, it was a tough day, but we got you there in time. It was a sad day. But Gordon, let me say I'm so proud of Patrick. Yes, it was a sad day, but you can be both. Sad and proud."

"Patrick, did you leave right after your physical?" I asked.

He answered, "No, a few weeks later. After I got the notice to report."

Patrick continued, "By the time I got the Selective Service Board notice to ship out, the first U.S. forces had already arrived in France in June 1917. As we sat by the fire, I read the notice to Pauline. We both knew this day would come, but until you actually have to face it, it doesn't feel real. Well, it became very real very quickly. We only had a couple of weeks together before I shipped out, and we had to decide what we were going to do."

Pauline touched Patrick's arm and said, "Well, I wanted to get married, but Patrick didn't want me to end up a widow in my twenties. When he said that, it struck me hard. I didn't want to lose him, but there were already so many men from here lying in the cemetery. Right over there, near the lake." She pointed to the right. Even before Patrick left for France, there were a few funerals for fallen soldiers. I knew all the widows. So, we decided to wait until he came home."

She put her hand on her chin, then said, "I remember one of them. His dad, I believe, was from Ireland too and knew my dad. His son was killed in the war. They were so proud of him. When he left for the war, he could barely read and write. But one day, they received a letter he had written all by himself. They said another soldier taught him how to read and write. Shortly after that letter, they were notified he had been killed in action. Heck, two of his younger brothers were killed in World War II. His parents passed away long ago, and the other siblings have all moved away. Tragically, their family lost so much in the wars."

Patrick wiped his bottom lip and said, "The day finally arrived when I was to be sworn in, and then I would head to the train for Basic Training. Pauline's father drove her and me. As I got up the steps for the train, I looked back at her and said…"

He stopped talking and lowered his head. I could see that what he was about to say weighed on him. His bottom lip started to quiver. Just as he was about to say something, Pauline said, "Patrick, I remember. I will never forget those words."

He lifted his head and said, "I love you and will see you soon. Gordon, people say that all the time, but I never thought it would be my last time seeing her beautiful face."

Pauline got up, knelt at his feet, and placed both of his hands on her face. He gently moved them from her forehead to her chin, seeing her with his hands. I was awestruck. As he felt her face, the smile on his face said it all. Their love was unmistakable. He placed his hands on the arms of his chair, got up, and walked into his house, Sarge right beside him. He crossed the threshold, turned, and didn't say a word. He didn't have to, as he walked into his house.

# CHAPTER 3

HIDDEN TALENT

As Pauline and I sat outside on the porch. The sound of someone playing the piano drifted from inside the house to the porch. I glanced at Pauline with a surprised expression, leaned forward, and asked, "Did Patrick put on a record?"

Laughing, she replied, "No, that's him playing."

I leaned back in my chair, listening intently as I tried to make out the song Patrick was playing. But it was not familiar. The music was captivating yet raw and deeply melancholic. Every key he struck and every note he played resonated with perfect pitch and rhythm.

Finally, I asked Pauline, "What song is that?"

"Hmm, he really doesn't play anyone else's songs. He can't read music, so he plays what's in his head. He tells me he plays what he sees."

"Did he play before going into the Army?"

"No, he never played before he went blind. His hidden talent was unlocked during his rehabilitation in an English hospital. One day, he heard someone playing and asked one of the attendants if he could give it a try. Of course, they agreed, hoping he would come out of his shell."

"So, he just went over to a piano and started playing like he is now? That's amazing."

She replied, "It truly is."

I responded, "He plays like a professional musician. How long will he play?"

"Yep, he is very good. How long depends on his mood. Sometimes, he plays so beautifully that I can close my eyes and get immersed in his playing. One time, after he was done, I asked him, 'What are you seeing as you play? He always replies, 'You, my dear, only you.' By the way, I have never heard him play so dark and gloomy. Based on what he is playing, I think you being here and your questioning has him conjuring up some unpleasant images from the past."

I asked, "Does he ever play in public?"

Pauline replied, "He did, for many years. He told me he wanted to let other blind veterans and the disabled know their lives were not over. But I'll tell ya, finding a job back then was almost impossible. There was a stigma attached to him and other veterans with visible injuries. They gave so much at such a young age. In their prime, it was like they were lepers. He became very resentful. It took some time for him to figure out what he wanted to do."

Suddenly, the music stopped just as abruptly as it had begun. Patrick and Sarge stepped back outside. He settled into his chair and said, "Gordon, what's your next question?"

"Patrick, I had one prepared, but I must ask how you play so beautifully. The song was captivating."

He didn't even acknowledge my remark regarding his playing. He just sat there silently and waited for the next question.

I leaned in and said, "What were the circumstances around your going blind?

Patrick cupped his face with his hands, rocked back, and said, "Pauline, you don't have to hear this if you don't want to. I'm afraid what I'm about to say will upset you. It's going to be brutal. Gordon knows, as I do, that war is not everything you see in the movies or on TV."

"Patrick, I'm here for you. I'm not going anywhere. I love you," she replied gently, squeezing his hand.

I asked, "Patrick, do you mind if I record this with my tape recorder? I'll also take notes, but I want to capture this on tape. I don't want to miss anything."

"No, not at all. I hope there is a lot of tape in there," he replied, smiling.

# CHAPTER 4



SOLDIERS HELPING SOLDIERS

It felt like Patrick's story took forever to begin. He removed his sunglasses, and I could see his eyes darting back and forth. We just sat there silently and waited. I didn't want to rush him. I could tell whatever story he was going to share weighed heavily on him.

"Gordon, before you ask your questions, I would like to talk about what I did when I got back. It will add to the entire story. Because what I will retell from the war will be hard to swallow or believe."

I pressed the record button on the tape recorder with my index finger and said, "Okay, Patrick." A click echoed as I started my tape recorder.

Patrick cleared his throat, took a deep breath, and exhaled. Nervously tapping his fingers on the arms of his chair, he leaned back, placed his hands behind his head, and clasped them together.

"I returned home in the late spring of 1919. Upon my return, there was no Veterans Administration. Here in Arkansas, I was fortunate to live relatively close to Fort Roots in North Little Rock. It is now part of the VA, but was previously a part of the Public Health Service hospital. We also had the Arkansas School for the Deaf and Blind and the Red Cross, which assisted soldiers returning home who were deaf, blind, or both. I applied the experience I gained in rehabilitation while in England, volunteering at both the Arkansas School for the Deaf and Blind and Fort Roots. I didn't limit my efforts to just veterans. I wanted to help everyone. It didn't matter to me who needed assistance. I wanted to contribute in any way I could. Initially, I would stay for about a week, as commuting was problematic. I would either take the bus or have someone give me a ride."

Pauline jumped in, "Long before World War II, I got my driver's license. We bought a used Model T, similar to the one my father had. He taught me how to drive, and I wanted the ability to take Patrick back and forth. I hated the thought of him being on the bus alone. Let's see, that was, I believe, in 1924."

Pauline got up and said, "Hold on for a minute. I'm going to grab something out of the house."

Patrick and I sat in silence, waiting for Pauline to return.

After a few minutes, Pauline walked out of the house with a large photo album. She sat back down and opened it. Patrick, hearing the pages turn, said, "Pauline, you didn't get the picture album, did ya?"

Smiling, she didn't respond.

"Gordon, look here."

I got up from my chair and leaned over Pauline.

Pointing to a picture, she said, "There's Patrick in front of Fort Roots. It was 1939 or 40. Standing next to him is Governor Bailey, and beside him is John Fordyce. He had just gotten an award from the Governor for volunteering at Fort Roots."

I stood up and said, "I know Governor Bailey, but who is John Fordyce?"

Patrick yelled, "What? Why have you ever gone to Camp Robinson? He was the designated construction engineer for the twelfth divisional cantonment that built Camp Robinson."

Before I could respond, Pauline turned the page. "Gordon, you will love this picture. This is Patrick and Elvis Presley at a club here in Bald Knob, called the Wagon Wheel, around 1951 or 1952. I'm not sure. Some good friends of ours, J.C. and Ruby York, owned it at that time.

"Elvis Presley, he looks so young," I replied.

"He was, I believe, sixteen or seventeen. A few years before he got famous," she replied.

I was dumbfounded; they met Elvis Presley.

Pauline continued and turned the page, "Here, look at this one. It was taken just last year or the year before. It's me, Patrick, and Governor Rockefeller. We attended one of his fundraising BBQs in Hot Springs when he was running for Governor; it was a lot of fun. Patrick played the piano, and there was a group of veterans there, and he came out of his shell for a brief period."

"Pauline, what I remember is that it was hot that day. Hot as can be," said Patrick.

Patrick paused for a moment and said, "I stopped volunteering full-time a couple of years ago. The back-and-forth was taking a toll on me. But, every once in a while, I received calls asking me to go down to the VA hospital in Little Rock to help one of the returning soldiers from Vietnam. Heck, if Pauline and I had kids, our grandkids would be off fighting in Vietnam. I felt compelled to help those young men and sometimes women when they got home. It was the least I could do for them."

"Patrick or Pauline, you don't have any kids?" I asked.

Pauline looked down and replied, "We had a little boy, Dauane. Whooping cough killed him. After that, I was not able to have any more children."

Patrick got up and slowly walked over to Pauline, feeling his way. He went over to her, put his arms around her, and said, "I love you! Always have and always will."

When he released her, I could see tears running down her cheeks. I wasn't sure whether it was from losing a child or the love both of them had for each other."

She wiped the tears from her eyes and said, "All those young men and women that Patrick helped, those are our kids."

I smiled and asked, "Do you have any idea how many veterans you have helped over the years?"

Rubbing his chin, he replied, "You know, Gordon, I have no idea. But I remember all of them. I just never wanted to count them."

He leaned forward and continued, "What I did, I did because it needed to be done. The Lord gave me a gift, and I put it to use. You can say I have been paying back a debt."

Pauline and I exchanged glances. Not once in the fifty years since Patrick had returned from the war had he ever mentioned repaying a debt as the reason he helped so many soldiers. She wondered, to whom?

Again, I asked, "Patrick, do you want to know how many you helped?"

"No, not really. I do know that in my seventy-one years on God's green earth, there have been too many." He took his sunglasses off, put them in his pocket, and wiped tears from his eyes. "I'll be right back," Pauline said, closing the album. She stood up and placed one hand on Patrick's shoulder before going inside to return the album.

# CHAPTER 5

THE HOMECOMING

Pauline walked out of their home, and I said, "You only left out a key detail, Patrick."

"What was that?" he replied.

"What about your wedding?" I asked.

Holding Pauline's hand, he replied, "Well, if you can imagine, the opportunities for a blind man in 1919 were slim to none. Her father didn't want us to get married. It's not that he didn't like me, but he didn't think I could support us. Well, honestly, I couldn't."

Pauline interrupted with fire in her voice, "Before I get to our wedding, I found out Patrick was wounded by his parents. I went over to visit them one day, and his dad was sitting outside their house with his head in his hands. He was holding a letter in one hand. Once I saw the letter, I ran to him and assumed the worst. Patrick had been killed. When I got to him, he just looked up with tears in his eyes and handed me the letter as he mumbled, 'My boy, Patty, has been wounded.' Throughout the years I knew his father, I never saw him cry before or after receiving the letter. He was a very hard individual. I took the letter and started to read it:

**To Mr. and Mrs. King, Bald Knob, Arkansas, War Department. I regret to inform you that Private Patrick W. King was wounded in battle. He is currently at Base Hospital 21, London, England, where his injuries are being treated. I will provide further updates as soon as possible. War Department.**

There was no mention of his wound or what he was being treated for. I asked him if he wanted me to write a letter on his behalf. He or Patrick's mom couldn't write and could barely read. He nodded, and I took a pen and paper out of my purse and started to write. Once we were done, I took the letter to the post office, which also had a telegram office, and sent it to Patrick, hoping he was still there. I checked back with his parents every couple of days, hoping they had heard from him, but I got no response. I was losing hope that he would return to me. He wasn't writing them or me."

Patrick interrupted, "I got the letter, and one of the nurses—I think her name was Claire... I forgot her last name—I asked her to read it to me, and she asked if I wanted to respond. I said no, but she would come back every day and ask me. I had a lot of thinking to do."

Pauline continued, "I didn't know what to think. All I knew was that Patrick was still in the hospital. I continued to write him, just as I did when he left for the Army. It wasn't until his parents showed me another letter they had received, stating that Patrick would be returning to America and discharged from the Army, and that he would arrive in Bald Knob by train sometime in late spring 1919. A more exact time would be provided once his out-processing was completed. I didn't know why he was not returning my letters, but I was determined to get that answer when he got home. If he didn't want to be with me anymore, I wanted him to say it to me. I still loved him, and in my heart, I knew he still loved me."

Patrick interrupted, "I still loved her, but I didn't want her to feel obligated to take care of a grown man... a blind grown man. She was so young, I wanted her to have a full life, not be a nurse to me."

Pauline stood up and said, "You were selfish and had no right to make that decision for me. I was a grown woman and would make my own decisions."

Pauline sat back down and continued, "Patrick's dad let me know that Patrick would be arriving on the 18th of April at 2:35 p.m. on the Missouri Pacific train from Little Rock. I asked my dad to drive to Patrick's parents' place to pick them up so we could go to the train station. Patrick's mother didn't want to go. Ever since they got the letter about him being wounded, she had shut down. Well, we all drove to the station and waited. As usual, the train was a little late.

The train stopped, and I could see all the soldiers standing and waving out of the windows. The doors opened, and everyone exited the train. I was shocked when some of the soldiers got off the train; some were still wearing bandages, and others were missing limbs. I honestly wasn't ready for what I saw. There was no sign of Patrick. We continued to wait. I started walking down the train looking for him. Almost panicking, I feared he had missed the train or decided not to come home. As I got closer to the last car, one of the porters was helping a soldier off the train, guiding him down the stairs. When they got off, the porter leaned in and said something to the soldier, then moved into position to walk down the train platform. The soldier nodded and, with a white cane in his right hand, started walking toward me. Now, at that time, I wasn't sure what the white cane was for, as the blind didn't commonly use it until the 1930s and 1940s.

When I got closer, I could see it was Patrick. I started to run toward him. I was, I guess, no more than fifteen feet away when I started yelling, 'Patrick, Patrick.' He couldn't hear me over all the sounds of the train's whistle. I thought to myself, *was he deaf?* By the time I got to him, he was walking down the platform next to the train, moving the cane side to side. He walked right past me. I froze. I knew then what his injuries were. I was pretty sure he was blind. It wasn't till later that I knew for sure. I turned around, then walked toward him and said, 'Patrick King, you stop right now!'

He stopped, turned in the direction of my voice, and said, 'Pauline,

Pauline, please leave. I'm not the man I was when I left. I'm blind. You loved that other man.'

I couldn't believe he just said that to me. I replied, 'You listen to me, Patrick Wayne King. I see the man I fell in love with. I see the man who fought for his country, and now I see the man I'm going to marry. So, never again tell me you're not the same man. Whatever the future brings, we will do it together. Now hug me.'

He dropped the big green bag he was carrying with his free hand, dropped his cane, and opened his arms. As we embraced, he said, 'I'm sorry, I'm sorry. It's going to be hard.'

I asked, 'Sorry for what? I love you and always will.'

He replied, 'I'll never see your beautiful face again.'

I said, 'Good, you won't see me age and turn into an old lady.'

He started to laugh and said, 'I love you, Pauline. Will you marry me? I need you.' Without any hesitation, I said, 'Yes, I'm the one who needs you.' From that day till now, we have been together."

Patrick interjected, "Well, her father was not too happy she was marrying me."

"Patrick, that is right, but I told my dad, Patrick was the man I was going to spend the rest of my life with, and if he disapproved, well, so be it. My daddy looked at me and replied, 'Honey, I know you love him, but love will not put food on the table or pay the bills. Come to your senses.' I just looked at him and walked off. Heck, I didn't talk to him or my mother for about a month. Eventually, both of them came to the same conclusion: I was going to marry Patrick. We worked things out, and they loved Patrick. They loved Patrick like a son. They both passed right before World War II, just months apart."

Patrick said, "They were good people." He looked over to Pauline and smiled.

I interrupted, saying, "Pauline, how were you going to provide for you and Patrick?"

She smiled and replied, "Honestly, I didn't know at that time. When Patrick went off to war, I attended college at Galloway Female College in Searcy. It's no longer there, but it was a great school. I had aspired to be a teacher, but when he got home, I quit after finding out he was blind. I couldn't let Patrick be alone. I needed to be there for him. Thus, I never finished all the requirements. His mom and dad were of no help. There was no way they could take care of him. So, I took a chance and applied to be a teacher here in Bald Knob. I knew they were shorthanded and needed teachers. Well, as luck would have it, the principal was a member of my church, and he hired me on the condition that I complete my requirements within a year. I loved teaching. I just retired a few years ago."

"Hold on, Pauline, you were the principal of the elementary school when you retired. Now she tutors some of the children from the town who are in need. An education is their only way to succeed." Patrick said proudly.

"Yes, but I was always a teacher at heart. So, after getting the job, we got married, and the rest is history, and we have been happily married for forty-nine years," she replied.

Seeing Pauline and Patrick, I thought to myself, *This is what true love must look like, and I hope I will have it one day.*

# CHAPTER 6

IN THE FIGHT

As they finished their conversation about their marriage, Patrick said, "I guess it's time to tell my story." I wondered, was it more of a journey? Pauline quietly settled back in her chair, pulled a handkerchief from her blouse, and listened with anticipation as he began to share it.

"I'll provide some background to help you fully understand what happened. My unit landed in France in late May 1918. It didn't take long for us to get into combat, which was fine with me and the others. The sooner we got into the fight, the sooner we would be home. We didn't fully grasp the extent of the war. We were naive. That was until we started moving to the front and started to see soldiers being transferred back to the rear with head bandages, bloody, covered wounds, some missing legs and arms. There were endless columns of soldiers carrying wounded soldiers on stretchers. For the more severely wounded soldiers, there were ambulances. Some were horse-drawn, while others were transported on trucks to hospitals away from the front lines. As they drove away from the front lines, an equal number of empty ones were moving toward the battlefield. It was neither I nor any of us who were ready for what was about to come. It was even worse once we reached the front and witnessed the death and destruction firsthand.

We lost four of the soldiers who were with us in the first week on the frontlines. I tell you, there were a million other places we would have preferred to be. It's not just the sights of war but the carnage that war brought to the people of Europe. It's the smell of burnt flesh, rotting bodies, gunpowder, and smells I can't even describe, but I can still smell them. The sheer destruction is unimaginable. Once, picturesque towns with beautiful, ornate buildings were reduced to rubble, and streets were littered with debris. You must see it for yourself. I'm not even sure pictures could tell the real story. I will never forget the sounds, which will stay with me forever. I remember when I got back home, I heard a car backfire; I dove to the ground. I heard folks say, 'What the hell is wrong with Patrick?' I thought, *nothing you can see*. Pauline grabbed my hand and helped me up, and we continued on our way.

Pauline asked me what had happened. I told her I tripped over the curb and fell. I didn't want to say I still had the sounds of war in my head."

He paused for a moment and was about to continue when Pauline leaned in, took his hand, and said, "I knew he didn't trip, but if there were something he wanted to tell me, he would. I just wanted him to know I was there then, and I'm here now."

As I listened to Patrick talk about the invisible injuries sustained by soldiers, I was deeply moved. I knew, too, that I had experienced them, but like him, I never discussed them. Like many veterans, I suppressed and compartmentalized these feelings in my mind. However, when Patrick spoke, his words resonated with me, sending my mind racing back to a French field in the fall of 1944.

Pauline noticed that I was starting to sweat and become agitated. "Gordon, are you okay?" she asked.

"Yes, I'm fine. Patrick, please continue."

Pauline got up and walked over to me, wrapping her arms around me in a bear-like hug as she whispered in my ear, "It's okay. Would you like a glass of lemonade? It's fresh. I just made it right before you got here."

She had seen the same look on Patrick's face many times over the years. She didn't know if it was guilt, remorse, or pain, or perhaps all three. She didn't know, nor could she fathom, what he or any other veteran was experiencing. All she knew was that she was there for him, and if someone were needed to support him, she would be that person.

Pauline got up and walked into the house. As she entered, it seemed she heard what I was saying to Patrick. She couldn't make it out. Maybe that was for the better. She took her time getting the lemonade.

I turned off my tape recorder.

"Patrick, can I ask you something?"

"Yes, of course. What's on your mind, young fella?"

"Does it get any easier?"

He knew exactly what I was asking. He replied, "No, no, it doesn't. You must find an outlet and come to terms with what happened, what you were ordered to do, and the things you saw. For me, God, my music, and helping fellow veterans bring me peace. My war was fifty years ago, and I'm an old man. Your war was just over twenty years ago. Your wounds are fresh. I can't imagine what the guys and gals coming back from Vietnam are going through.

We had days, maybe even weeks, to distance ourselves from the war, and a great nation welcomed us home. Today, one day, they are in the rice paddies, killing and watching their buddies getting killed. The next day, they are in the States and have no homecoming. If anything, they are being called baby killers or worse. If there is such a thing. I hate it. Just think, the average age of soldiers in our wars was twenty-six; today, it's twenty-two. It seems the young will always pay the price for freedom. Don't get me started on the Korean War."

I sat there for a bit before I replied, "I know. My step-brother was a grunt in the 9th Infantry Division. He was wounded, but he is okay now. He doesn't talk about it either."

Patrick asked, "What is it about us veterans?"

I thought about his question, but I had no answer.

"It makes me mad that everyone forgot about that one. It was our first test against the Communists. I'm glad your brother is okay. What's his name?"

I replied, "Mark, and boy, he's smart! When he got out of the Army, he used his G.I. Bill to earn his Bachelor's Degree in Physics from LSU and a Master's Degree in Astrophysics from Texas Tech."

"You sound very proud of him," Patrick said as he slapped my knee.

I smiled and said, "Yep, I'm proud of my little brother."

When Patrick spoke, the passion in his voice was palpable, and his anger felt sincere. He paused, and we remained silent for what seemed like an eternity. Suddenly, he took my hand and asked, "Will you pray with me?"

I took his hand and replied, "Yes, I would like that, but I'm not religious."

He smiled and said, "I wasn't either, but there are no atheists in a foxhole."

I squeezed his hand a little firmer. He started praying, "Oh God, we humbly ask for your protection. Guard us, our brothers and sisters, from harm. Grant us the strength to face each challenge and the peace of mind to carry on. May we return home safely, and always remember to be grateful for the blessings we have. Amen."

"If you'd like to talk, please don't hesitate to let me know. I'm here. I truly believe that speaking in a group with other veterans helps. Even if it's a group of two."

With a nervous laugh, I replied, "Thank you, Patrick. I'm going to take you up on that."

"I see you two are getting along. Okay, everyone, the lemonade is ready. Who wants one?" Pauline asked as she bolted out the door. She had waited inside until she heard the end of Patrick's and my prayer.

We both replied, "Fill them up, please," as I held Patrick's and my glasses for her to fill. I gave Patrick his glass and said, "Pauline and Patrick, thank you for your hospitality."

When Patrick started to talk, I turned on my tape recorder.

Patrick took a long drink, put the glass down, and said, "Just after midnight on July 9th, 1918, German commandos crossed the Marne River in small boats just to the south of our position. The chaos wrought was a morale buster. We all felt vulnerable. The havoc they created was vivid in our minds. The commandos had severed communication lines, breached the defenses, and killed a dozen U.S. soldiers, all without losing a single commando. To say the least, the American commanders were caught off guard. Even before the sun began to rise, we started to hear rumors that the commanders felt compelled to conduct a risky raid against the Germans inside their lines.

However, the German shelling was relentless, leaving us no way to carry out a raid. I mean, the thunder from the German artillery barrage had been deafening—a mix of conventional and gas shells. The dead soldiers littered the battlefield, and the wounded were being treated at the makeshift hospital located to our rear. For the brief times the shelling subsided, we would go over the trench and retrieve our dead. The only thing we had to watch out for was the German machine guns. They were deadly. There's something to be said about a man risking his life to help another man he may not know, to ensure that he is dead, and to bury him in a proper grave. Even during the war, some civilized behavior was observed. Well, this day was no different as the shells began to strike, painting the sky with an orange-red hue that seemed to glow.

My company's position was along the banks of the Marne River near Château-Thierry. The Marne River lies to the east-southeast of Paris. It's a tributary of the Seine that flows from Paris to Langers, about 319 miles from its source to its end. We were only about sixty miles from Paris, which is remarkably close when you consider the distance German artillery could fire. I even heard reports of parts of Paris receiving German artillery. If the Germans had managed to cross the Marne, they could have reached Paris quickly and possibly won the war. After all, it only took a few weeks when they invaded France in mid-May of 1940."

As Pauline and I listened intently, Patrick closed his eyes. It was as if he were there, reliving it fifty years later. He took a drink of his lemonade and continued, "As the sun rose, a heavy fog settled over the river. I once imagined the river as a beautiful sight, with green, grassy banks, walkways along the shore, couples in rowboats, beautiful water-powered mills, and children playing along the shores, before the war. But that wasn't how it was during the war. It was full of debris, wood, metal, and, yes, bodies floating down the river. Most, if not all, of the ancient bridges were destroyed. The Germans or we would build makeshift bridges, but they wouldn't last long before being destroyed.

The water wasn't blue or even brown. It was black, and the odor was overwhelming. With the heavy fog, we couldn't see the other side, but we could hear a lot of activity. We had been warned of a possible German attack for days, but so far, only commando raids and artillery rounds had rained down on us. They were preparing for the battlefield and trying to kill or wound as many as possible before the ground attack. We all knew it. We just waited in the trenches. The trenches were a miserable place, with mud everywhere; the stench was almost unbearable, and there were rats. The trenches were built by the Germans years before when they occupied this side of the Marne. World War I was a war of feet and inches. The battle lines might have shifted a few miles, but not to the extent of World War II.

Now, occasionally, they would fly their planes over our positions and drop a bomb or two. That was the damnedest thing. Luckily, they were not accurate, but if you were in the spot where the bombs landed, they could be devastating and cause more psychological torment. As the shells landed once again, we ducked into the trenches. Then we heard the warning signal for a gas attack and quickly put on our gas masks. It was much easier when we were in those god-awful trenches, mainly because we were stationary. However, putting one on while running is challenging. If you were in the open and stopped to put it on, you would be killed by machine gun fire. Stopping on the battlefield was the worst thing a soldier could do. Still, it can be done, and I practiced putting it on while running. You didn't go anywhere without your gas mask—nowhere, not even when you took a shower or used the latrine. Gordon, did you have to wear a gas mask in World War II?"

I replied, "We had them, but I never wore mine, and I didn't know anyone who did in my unit. We would use it as a pillow while we waited on the flight line to man our planes. I think after the effects of gas in the Great War, no one wanted to use it. Most of the time, we used them as pillows. Hell, Hitler was a victim of a gas attack in World War I."

Patrick shifted in his chair, took a sip of lemonade, and continued, "Based on the rumors we heard and the commando raid the other night, we pretty much knew the Germans were about to launch a massive offensive, putting us in direct danger. As the shells rained down, some distance to our left, the signal for a possible gas attack sounded. My platoon sergeant grabbed Corporal Johnston, my squad leader. While they ran down the trench, Corporal Johnston turned and said, 'Keep your eyes focused in front of you. I'll be right back.'

That was the last time any of us saw him as he and the platoon sergeant continued down the trench. I put my gas mask on. I stood up and stepped onto the wooden walkway, allowing me to see over the berm into No Man's Land with a periscope, which let us see ahead without exposing ourselves. I heard the whistling sound of a shell coming in and saw a blast off to my right as it exploded. Then I felt the concussion from the explosion. It almost blew me off the walkway. A dust plume flew past me, and I couldn't see a foot in front of my face. Dust was everywhere. When it cleared, I stepped down from the walkway and looked down the trench in the direction the platoon sergeant and squad leader had gone. I didn't hear all the 'all-clear signals.' I looked around, and everyone had their masks, so I took off mine and didn't realize I was the only one still wearing a gas mask. I have grown accustomed to wearing it when artillery rained down on us."

Patrick took a deep breath and continued, "I could taste the picric acid from the German explosives. I told the soldier next to me, a good buddy of mine, Private Larsen, also known as Lar. We met in basic training and have been together since then, and we're pretty close to each other. I knew I could trust him, and he knew I had his back. It's remarkable how the Army can bring together individuals who are so different, form them into a cohesive team, and foster trust like no other. I think that is what I miss about the Army. Hell, he was from Pittsburgh, Pennsylvania, and I was a sharecropper from Bald Knob, Arkansas. He told me before the war that he had worked at a steel mill, just like his dad. Some of his stories were so funny; he was a funny guy, the kind of guy you need in combat. Heck, I think I was one of the few from the South; most of the unit was from the Northeast."

Patrick halted and cleared his throat.

"He was a great guy."

I didn't want to ask him what happened to Lar. I figured he would have said it already or would say it later.

"Well, I told Lar I was going to check on them. I then ran toward them. When I got there, I couldn't do anything. Their bodies were peppered with shrapnel. I leaned over the corporal and felt for a pulse, but there was none. Then, I moved over to the platoon sergeant, again, nothing. They were both dead. I just knelt there when I heard, 'Private, get your ass back to your station.' I looked up, and there was the company commander, blood running down his face, pointing in the direction down the trench. I got up and ran back, not looking behind. I didn't need to see any more death. I knew there would be plenty in the days to come."

Patrick stood up, took Sarge by his leash, and stepped off the porch. Pauline and I remained seated in silence as he walked away.

He turned around and said, "Corporal Johnston was a good man and an excellent leader. His wife was a young widow."

I turned off the recorder. We waited for Patrick to return. In the background, we could hear Sarge barking. He must have taken off his harness to free himself from his duties and chase squirrels. Based on his barking, he must have treed one or more.

After a few minutes, Patrick and Sarge returned to the porch and sat down again. "Sorry, I just needed to clear my head. I love walking,

Sarge, and he needed to go to the bathroom and run for a bit. Let me see, where was I?"

"Before we start, Patrick, how long have you had Sarge?" I asked.

"Well, he is my third Sarge. I got him in June 1966, right, Pauline?"

"Yes, Patrick, it was right around my birthday."

"Patrick, please continue when you want." As he began to talk, I started my recorder.

"It didn't take long for our squad to merge with another that was short on personnel. We didn't have many replacements at that time. There were many soldiers in the field hospitals sick with the Spanish flu. Well, at the time, we didn't have a name for it, only 'influenza.' I got lucky and never had it, or I was asymptomatic.

Along with the remaining members of my platoon, I was assigned to the third platoon. They were right next to us in the trench, so we didn't have to move, just new NCOs to yell at us. Lar and I were assigned to the 2nd squad. We both knew the squad leader. We met him in basic training, so the transition was pretty easy.

As Corporal Stevens walked up to me, he put out his hand, and we shook. He said, 'Patty, glad to have you and Lar in the squad. You know most of the guys in the squad. You can introduce Lar to anyone he doesn't know, but you know most of them. There are a couple of new guys. You two take up a position left of Scotty.'

I replied, 'Roger, to the left of Scotty, and let's get this war over.' He didn't reply, just walked off. For him, that was not normal. Something about him was odd, or perhaps 'off' is a better way to put it. He seemed distracted, almost in a daze. I surely wasn't going to ask him. One: the last few days were stressful; two: he was an NCO. Even though I knew him, I didn't think it was my place. It didn't take us any time to assimilate into the squad. We really didn't have time to assimilate. The war was not going to stop, so we could get to know each other.

The Germans continued their shelling throughout the day and into the early evening. We were all exhausted, and with little sleep, Lar and I lay on wooden pallets next to each other as we waited in our muddy, foul-smelling trenches, clutching our rifles and gas masks as we anticipated the waves of German infantry that would soon attack our positions."

I interrupted him and asked, "Patrick, can you describe the trenches?"

He shuffled his feet on the porch as if he were trying to move something.

"The trenches were a maze cut into the ground. The mud in northern France is clay-like, and when it gets wet, it never dries and becomes sticky. It sticks to everything. Our boots would weigh twice as much with all the mud."

I looked down, and he rubbed his shoes together, reliving the past right in front of Pauline and me. He wasn't even aware he was doing it.

"You could easily get lost trying to navigate from one to another. Most had names resembling cities or streets, like Main, First, Maple, Elm, and, of course, Second. Along the walls of many were wooden planks for structural support and sandbags for stability, which were filled not with sand but with dirt. They were nine to twelve feet deep, with duckboards on the floor to keep your feet dry, but I'll tell you, when it rained—and it often did—your feet would still get wet. On top of the trenches were more sandbags and barbed wire. Along the walls of the trenches, there were what we called fire steps, which we would climb to fire at the Germans. When we had to go out and over the trenches, we would put a wooden ladder against the wall and climb."

Patrick's voice started to tremble. "Normally, the first couple of guys over were okay, but once the Germans saw us coming over, they would open up with their machine guns. It was a bloodbath, even with some soldiers falling back into the trench, including the one you just talked to. However, I didn't see anyone ever hesitate when it was their turn to go out of the trenches.

When you got out of the trenches and reached the rolls of wire, there would be soldiers slung over the wire. I'm not even sure if I ever stopped or slowed down to see who it was. All I knew was I didn't want to be one of them. I didn't want to die in No Man's Land.

Everyone else and I would step over them or sometimes walk on them to get over the wire. We continued to attack. The first rule was never to stop moving forward—that is what the Germans wanted, for us to stop moving and become stationary targets. A soldier running is harder to hit, but once over, we just kept running, zigzagging, trying not to get killed. I had so many friends get mowed down. You could hear the ping, ping when a round hit a helmet. There was not much you could do for them. Once the machine guns started, the mortar rounds would begin to impact."

As Patrick spoke, I glanced over at Pauline. Her eyes said it all, tears running down her cheeks. She had never heard him speak in this manner. When he talked, it was as if he were running and almost out of breath. His head moved from side to side as though he were watching his fellow soldiers fall next to him. Suddenly, he stopped and caught his breath. He turned his head in Pauline's direction and said, "I'm sorry, dear. I never wanted you to hear any of this. Gordon, I think I'm done. I'm putting Pauline through too much pain."

Pauline stood up and knelt beside Patrick, placing her hands on his knees as she said, "I want you to finish. You need to finish; I'm tougher than you think." She kissed his cheek and said, "I love you."

# CHAPTER 7



Pauline glanced at her watch and said, "Patrick, it's already eleven thirty. Gordon, please join us for lunch. It's not much. I'll make some bologna and cheese sandwiches. Oh, I think we have some chips, too."

I leaned forward and answered, "Pauline, I never thought it would take this long. I don't want to impose. But honestly. I didn't pack a lunch, so if it's okay with Patrick, I would love to have lunch with you."

Patrick laughed so hard that his eyes began to water. He slapped his knee and said, "Gordon, I had hoped by now you would know that Pauline pretty much runs this place. There's no way I would say you can't join us for lunch. If I did, I would be leaving with you."

Pauline got up, bent over, kissed Patrick on the cheek, and whispered, "Finally, after fifty years, you admit it."

"I'll make the sandwiches. Gordon, mustard, or mayo. What about cheese?"

I replied, "Yes, the cheese and mustard always go with bologna, and thank you."

Patrick and Pauline nodded their heads in unison.

While Pauline was in the kitchen preparing the sandwiches, I stood up, walked down the porch, and said, "You have a lovely home, Patrick. It's so quiet and peaceful. It's not like my one-bedroom apartment in Little Rock. I miss having a yard."

"Thank you, Gordon. Can I ask you something? If I'm out of line, please let me know."

"Sure, Patrick, and don't worry."

"So I take it, you're not married? What happened?"

I sat back down and replied, "I was married. After the war, I moved back home, met a beautiful young lady, and fell in love."

"Where is home?"

"Dallas is where my mom and stepfather moved to from the East Coast in the mid-twenties. They both are gone now, first my mom, then my stepfather. When I returned from the war, all I wanted was to get married and raise a family."

"Stepfather, what happened to your biological father?"

"From what my mom told me, he was killed in France in mid-October 1918. I was very young when he went off to fight, and I never saw him again. My mom would talk about him, and honestly, I don't even remember what my last name was. Grover is my stepfather's name."

Patrick rubbed his chin and said, "That would have been during the Meuse-Argonne offensive, also known as the Fall Offensive. Do you know where he is buried? Why didn't you tell me earlier that your father fought in the Great War?"

I nodded my head and replied, "Good question. I don't discuss him often because I really didn't know him well. It was so long ago. My mom told me she thinks he is buried in France, but she was never sure since he was listed as missing in action. As far as I know, he was never found, or his body recovered."

"Okay, so you got married, and well, what happened?"

"Janette, that's her name, wanted to settle down. Remember when I mentioned I wanted to get married and have a family? We got married after dating for a few months, and a few years later, we had a son. April 18th, 1949, to be exact."

I got up and started to pace. "I took a job as an insurance salesman. I felt trapped and quite bored. I missed flying, so I applied for a pilot position at American Airlines out of Love Field. I think I missed the adrenaline rush of flying. I got the position and loved it, but traveling and being away from home put a real strain on our relationship. Being apart all the time, we grew apart and eventually decided to split and get a divorce. A commercial pilot's schedule is grueling. She and my son still live in Dallas. Well, when he is not in school, that is. Hell, he had to register for the draft last year. But right now, he is a Sophomore at the University of Texas at Austin and joined the Army ROTC program to help pay for school."

Patrick asked, "So he wants to go into the Army? Even with the war in Vietnam."

"Yep, I tried to talk him out of it, but he was determined."

"Hmm, okay. So, why don't you fly anymore?" Patrick asked.

I stood there and didn't answer for a couple of minutes. I walked to the edge of the porch and replied, "I moved to Little Rock ten years ago and went to work for the paper." I then turned around and sat back down in my chair. No more than a minute passed before we heard Pauline's voice, "Get in here. Lunch is ready."

We all sat at the kitchen table in silence, processing the conversations that had taken place. Pauline got up and asked, "Patrick, can I take your plate?"

He replied, "Yep, I'm done, and thank you."

She looked at me, and I nodded. She then picked up my clean plate. There wasn't a bread crumb or a piece of potato chip on it.

As she walked over to the sink, I said, "No, Ma'am, let me get those dishes, and a bologna sandwich has never tasted better."

She replied, "Why don't you guys go back outside. This will only take a second."

"Shall we go back outside and continue our conversation?" Patrick asked.

I walked out of the kitchen and replied, "Of course, if you are up to it."

"Gordon, my boy, you've opened a can of worms that I can't close," Patrick said as Sarge assisted him back out to the porch.

"Come on, Gordon, let's get this show on the road!" Patrick yelled from the porch.

I looked at Pauline and said, "I think we'd better get out there before he changes his mind."

She grabbed me by the arm and said, "Way ahead of you." We both sat down and waited for Patrick to start up again. When he did, I activated my recorder.

Patrick took a deep breath.

# CHAPTER 8



A warm southern breeze blew across the porch, and the rustling of the trees could be heard in the distance. The sound was very relaxing. Pauline and I waited for Patrick to start speaking.

"As we ate chow, we were replaced by the 3rd squad while we ate. As we all sat together, the commanding figure of First Sergeant Gibbs joined us, along with the Commanding Officer, Captain Bertinetti, who walked over. We were about to get up, but Captain Bertinetti said, 'At ease, don't get up.' He motioned for Corporal Stevens. He got up and walked over to them, and as they talked, they moved away from us. Corporal Stevens turned, and I could see on his face that he was not happy with the direction of the conversation. All three walked back, and Captain Bertinetti said, 'I have some great news, Corporal Stevens has been promoted to Sergeant and will be taking over 3rd Platoon. However, not until next week.'

We all got up and shook his hand. I don't think he was pleased about leaving the squad, but he deserved it. We all wondered who would take over the squad. We were also given a warning order for an upcoming mission briefing and told to be at the Company Command Post at 2155 for our mission briefing.

After the First Sergeant and CO left, the newly promoted Sergeant Stevens said, 'Patty, Lar, Willy, Rusty, and Scotty. The five of you will accompany me on the mission. The rest of you guys will be with the 1st squad till we get back. You five meet back here at 2140. Only bring your rifle and gas masks. We will come back here after the briefing.'

Patrick put his hands together and placed them on his lap, saying, "As Sergeant Stevens walked off, he took what looked like an envelope and looked at it. He saw me see him, put it in his pocket, turned around, and slowly walked off."

* * *

"It was 2140, and we were all assembled. With Sergeant Stevens in the lead, we moved down the trench to the Command Post, which was merely a cave carved into the trench wall and supported by wooden beams. Sergeant Stevens entered first, and we all followed. The room was lit by kerosene lamps, casting a warm glow, odd for a trench. The CO, 1st SGT, and a couple of other soldiers were already in the CP. I noticed a large map on the wall. The map displayed the locations of U.S. and French forces, as well as those of the Germans. I could only speculate how we knew their locations. I guessed it was from the prisoners we had captured and reconnaissance missions. We were all instructed to take a seat. As we settled in, an officer walked in—someone I didn't recognize. What was odd about him was that he didn't have any rank on his collar."

I interrupted Patrick and asked, "So, how did you know he was an officer?"

He smiled and answered, "Officers' uniforms were a little different. They had more buttons and pockets on their tunics and fit better than the enlisted. I had never seen him before he walked into the dugout, but when he arrived, everyone stood at attention, which was another giveaway.

He said, 'At ease, sit down and relax.' I thought, *"Relax. What the hell is that?"* Lar and I sat next to each other. After a minute or two, the officer began a high-level briefing, providing an overview of the mission.

As he moved to the map on the dugout wall, he pulled out a pointer and said, 'Gentlemen, the German 7th Army is located here,' pointing to the location, 'and we are here. As you know, last night, their stormtroopers carried out numerous attacks on our positions using walking bridges they built across the river, here and here. These bridges allowed them to move quickly in and out. Since then, most have been taken out, but the remaining one we believe will be used to launch an offensive, and we have set up a machine gun nest to over-watch it.'

"He took a pause. 'However, tonight at midnight, a patrol led by Sergeant Stevens will conduct a reconnaissance on one of the Germans' rear command posts and verify troop and artillery place-ment located here. In addition to the reconnaissance, we want you to locate the communication lines going into the Command Post and cut them before moving to the pickup point.' He pointed to a location on the map. All our eyes widened. It was at least 10 miles behind their lines. I thought to myself, *how in the hell would we get that far without being detected?*

Well, I would soon have my answer. He continued his briefing, 'Sergeant Stevens, your squad will be going out of the trench and over the wire here, through a path that the engineers will cut, then reseal when you're through. You will then cross the river, using one of the German canvas boats we captured. Then, into No Man's Land, then behind their lines, pointing to a location on the map. Once you have linked up with our contact, he will guide you to the location. Once he does, continue your mission, conduct the reconnaissance, cut the wires, and then go to the rendezvous point.'

Pointing to a spot on the map, he said, 'Are there any questions? "No one said anything."

"He continued, 'Here at this location, you will link up with an infantry squad. They will be in a canvas boat to bring you back through our lines. You need to be at that location no earlier than 2340 and no later than 2355 tomorrow night. That will give you twenty-four hours or so to reach your objective, complete your mission, and get to the rendezvous point. You will need to work out the timeline to determine when to leave your Observation Post to arrive at the link-up at no later than 2355 tomorrow night. When you get within 100 yards, you will pop this flare.'

He handed Sergeant Stevens the two flares, smiling. Smiling, he turned and gave one to me and the other to Lar. We both looked at him and nodded our heads. 'Are there any questions?' he asked. Well, let me tell you, there were plenty. I could see it on the soldiers' faces, but no one said anything, not one word."

"As the briefer was about to speak, German artillery began to fall and impact very close to our location. This caused dirt to rain down from the ceiling, and all I heard was 'everyone out, out now!' I guess they were afraid of a cave-in. I mean, the artillery was that close. I could feel the earth move beneath my feet. It rattled my bones. Everyone got out and manned a position on the trench line, waiting for the imminent attack. I could hear the screams of wounded soldiers to my left and right. Stretcher bearers were running behind me in the trench, trying to get to the wounded soldiers. After a few minutes, the shelling stopped, and we were ordered back to the command post. I wasn't too keen on that idea, going into No Man's Land, but I couldn't say no. I was a soldier, and soldiers do what they are ordered to do as long as it is a lawful order."

I stopped Patrick and asked, "Are stretcher bearers the same as what we called medics or corpsmen?"

He nodded and said, "Yes, but the difference is stretcher bearers weren't medically trained. They could provide first aid, but their primary role was getting wounded soldiers to medical treatment. What drove them was the desire to help their fellow soldier."

Before he got a chance to continue, Pauline asked, "No Man's Land. Patrick, what is No Man's Land?"

"It's what we refer to as a barren, pot-marked strip of land or an area situated between our lines and the enemy. We would fight over it. One day, we owned it, and the next, they did. Essentially, it was a killing field. Typically, there would be nothing but bare land with broken and bare tree trunks—some tall, some short—and a few branches, but none with leaves. The artillery and machine guns took care of them. Then there were the shell craters everywhere. You couldn't walk a few feet without coming across one. Some were quite deep, and those made you stop for a bit to catch your breath or use them to fire at the Germans. The German machine guns couldn't hit you while you were in there. Often, there were dead soldiers or what was left of them in the craters."

Patrick took a deep breath through his nose and continued, "More often than not, they were filled with smelly, dirty, rat-infested water or mud that had its own kinda stench. Let me tell you, I have been around farms, livestock, manure, and fertilizer my entire life. It's nothing compared to the smell in shell craters. It was bad enough during the day, but at night, No Man's Land seemed to come alive. The noises you would hear kept you awake if you had the unfortunate luck of being stuck out there on a listening post. The noise I hated the most was the rats feeding on the dead soldier's flesh. You could hear them nibbling on the dead soldier's face, then running away when they were finished or startled. When a shell exploded above, the light would cast a shadow on whatever was still standing. The tree trunks cast the eeriest shadows. One night, I saw one that looked like a cross, but it was not in the Holy Land. No Man's Land was only death and despair. When the wind blew, the branches rubbed against each other, making a hollow sound. If emptiness had a sound, that is what it would sound like. If you can imagine hell on earth, it would be No Man's Land."

Patrick took a breath and sipped his lemonade.

"When we all got back in the Command Post, I looked around, glancing at the soldiers, and we all had one thing in common, and we knew it. What we had in common was that we were all going over the wire. We knew that night would be like no other. We didn't know who would make it home, if any of us."

I could hear Patrick tapping his fingers on the arms of his chair as if he were counting. Suddenly, he stopped, cleared his throat, and continued.

"Now, the officer continued his briefing, but this time it was very detailed.

'At 2330, your squad will go over the trench at this location and through the wire here at 2345.'

Sergeant Stevens took out his map and marked the location on it. 'The engineers will give you a six-minute window, either three minutes before or three minutes after. No more. If you are too early or late, you might be fired upon, so everyone, let's synchronize our watches.'

Everyone looked at their watches and was ready to sync. 'The time now is 2220.' My watch was only a couple of minutes off, but enough to get killed by friendly forces.

'Excuse me, sir, but have you timed how long it will take my squad to move from our position along the trench to the egress point?' Sergeant Stevens asked.

'Yes, my team has, and it will take ten minutes,' replied the briefer.

I thought to myself, *if you're running.*

He continued, 'You will move along the downward slope of the riverbank 200 yards to this location. At 2355, our artillery is going to open up with a barrage away from your location. We hope it will throw them off and cause them to concentrate their activities in that sector. The barrage will last for ten minutes, pounding the German lines. In coordination with the high explosives, another battery will create a smoke screen along the German side of the river.'

'Once the smoke screen commences, you will get into the canvas boat and make your way to the other side of the river. Again, it will be down the riverbank, but you should be able to see it as you move toward it. It is covered in a canvas tarp, with some brush to conceal it. Now, the smoke screen will remain in place for fifteen minutes. During that time, you must cross the river. At 2358, Sergeant Stevens, your patrol will begin crossing the Marne. Once you make it across, proceed to this location to meet our contact. At 0030, he will signal you with two flashes of white light, followed by one flash of red light.

You will return with two flashes of white light. After linking up with the contact, he will guide you through the German lines to your objective. He will not, I repeat, not accompany you to the objective. Conduct your reconnaissance, locate the communication lines, and cut them. You don't have to go all the way to it. We don't want you to make contact with the Germans. You would never survive.'

I thought to myself, *This sounds like a suicide mission.* He continued, 'This is a reconnaissance mission. Just close enough to find and cut the lines. Once you have completed that, move to this location.' He pointed it out on the map. 'There, you will be met by an infantry squad that will bring you back across the river. I can't tell you how vital your mission is. We have tried to hit it with artillery and by air, but it's defended and fortified. Our bombs or artillery can't penetrate it. The best we can hope for is that by cutting their communication lines, we might be able to delay their assault by a few hours.'

Sergeant Stevens asked, 'Do we link back up with our contact to guide us back?' With a stern face, he replied, 'Negative, we can't take the chance of the Germans knowing he works for us. I recommend moving as far and as fast as you can when it's dark and finding a place to hunker down during the day. I recommend you set up your OP here.' He pointed to a location on the map using his pointer.

'It will provide cover and concealment. In addition, it has a great field of sight on your objective.' It's a concrete building that the Germans use as an observation post. We have flown reconnaissance flights over it in the last few days, and we have not seen any activity around it. So, it should be a safe place for you and your patrol Sergeant Stevens. After your mission, proceed to the link-up point, which is marked again on the map. 'You pop the second flare. If you don't and try to move to the boat, it may not be pleasant for you. If you arrive at the pickup late and they are gone, and manage to make it back across the Marne, we will have lookouts waiting for you. Remember the one bridge we have eyes on. It's located here. Use this one. Do not. I repeat, do not use the flare—two flashes of your flashlight. Wait till you get three back, then move across in a single file.

I want to get back to the infantry squad. If you don't have your flair, use the sign and counter sign. We got wet. The reply is Come and get dry.'

Lar and I just looked at each other and didn't say a word. We had both been in battle before, but in my gut, I knew it was going to be different. I didn't realize how different it was at the time. I didn't say anything to Lar. I raised my hand and said, 'Sir, cross the Marne, go through No Man's Land, meet up with a spy, cut communication lines into a German command bunker, and make it back here by tomorrow night? Why don't we just hit it with artillery again and again?'

Without skipping a beat, he replied, 'Yes, soldier, the patrol you're a member of has been tasked with a challenging and critical mission. I didn't say it was going to be easy.' He never answered the artillery question.

We got the answer to my question when we got to OP. Looking down at his watch, he said, 'I suggest you and your fellow patrol members start to get ready. I think the hardest part is crossing the Marne in fifteen minutes.' He looked at me and asked, 'Do you still have the flare?"

I replied, 'Roger,' and showed it to him.

He said, '100 yards out, pop it.'

To him, there was nothing to it, just a stroll in the park. This soldier scared me. I didn't know what it was at the time, but he just did. Heck, he didn't even have the same unit patch as the one we all wore."

"Patrick, you didn't know at the time. What do you know now?" I asked.

"Well, while I was in the hospital, he stopped by to see how I was doing. I recognized his voice. I will never forget it. I told him I was not in the mood to chat, so he left. I asked the doctor who that was. He replied that it was Major General Dennis Noland, General Pershing's Senior Intelligence Officer. I must admit, even if I had known he was a general, I still wouldn't have wanted to talk to him. I was a tad bitter.

After the briefing, we all returned to our designated area in the trench. We cleaned our gear, checked the flashlight batteries, loaded magazines, and sharpened our knives and bayonets. Once we finished with our individual gear, each of us checked the others' gear. We all anxiously waited for the time to move out. Oh, I forgot. We were told not to tell anyone, no one at all."

Patrick, who was the person you linked up with on the German side?

"Gordon, I'll get to him in a bit."

# CHAPTER 9

OUT OF THE TRENCH

Just off the porch, the bushes started to sway in the afternoon breeze. I looked over at them, and bees were everywhere. I sat back and took a long, deep breath through my nose, taking in the scent of the air. It was soothing and filled with a beautiful fragrance.

I turned to Pauline and asked, "Where is that beautiful scent coming from?"

She replied, "I love the smell too. It comes from those bushes in front of the porch. They're called Confederate Jasmine. Well, I guess they are more of a vine than a bush. But I love the smell, I know it's summer when I smell them."

I replied, "Looks like the bees love them too." She smiled and batted one away from her face. While Pauline and I were talking, Patrick sat in his chair, not saying a word. Based on his breathing, he was enjoying the smell as much as, or more than, Pauline and I were.

He leaned forward and started talking again. "Once we got back to our position in the trench, Sergeant Stevens came up to me and said, 'I want you to walk at a normal pace with full gear from here to the egress point. I believe it will take longer than we were briefed.' I replied, 'Roger,' gathered my gear, and set off. When I got back, Sergeant Stevens was 100% accurate. It took fifteen minutes. Once he had that information, he adjusted our departure time and told everyone to be ready to move at 2310. With the time remaining before we started our mission, we tried to get some rest, but in the trenches, it's tough to do." I could hear Patrick's breathing increase as he spoke.

"At precisely 2310, Sergeant Stevens gathered us all together and arranged for us to move down the trench to the spot where we were going to go over the trench and through the wire. It was Willy, Rusty, Lar, and then me. Behind me was Sergeant Stevens, and in the rear was Scotty with the BAR, who would cover us if needed. Once we were lined up, we walked down the trench to our point of departure. It took exactly fifteen minutes. Sergeant Stevens tapped me on the shoulder and gave me a thumbs-up. When we arrived, we waited. No one said a word. If it weren't for the sound of artillery in the distance, you could have heard a pin drop. I couldn't remember a quieter time on the front. I wasn't sure if that was good or bad, but we were about to find out. I could feel my heart beating in my chest, one beat after another, thump, thump, thump. I knew I was alive as long as I could feel its rhythm."

"At 2330, Sergeant Stevens tapped me on the shoulder and raised two fingers. I nodded and tapped Lar on the shoulder, who then did the same to Rusty and Rusty to Willy. Willy then tapped Scotty. I had a lump in my throat that felt like the size of a baseball, and I could hardly swallow. My mouth was dry. Even though I had just taken a drink of water, I didn't know if I was scared, anxious, nervous, or all three. Sweat began to pour off my forehead. Good—it was dark, and there was plenty of cloud cover, which was beneficial since there was a waxing crescent moon. However, if the clouds drifted away, it would be dicey. I closed my eyes when suddenly, I felt a hand on my shoulder pushing me. I took my right hand and pushed Lar, who then pushed

Rusty, who then pushed Willy. Willy placed his right foot on the first rung of the ladder, then his left on the next, and he was out of the trench.

When it was my turn to exit, my foot slipped in the mud, and I almost fell back. Sergeant Stevens put his hand on my back and pushed me. I regained my balance, and within a few seconds, I was on the other side. I noticed I was breathing fast, so I tried to slow my breathing. After less than a minute, I was breathing normally, but my adrenaline was pumping. One by one, we went over the trench. As Scotty was almost out of the trench, the Germans popped multiple flares. They illuminated the entire battlefield. I didn't know if they detected us or if it was harassment, and I waited for the machine gunfire. We all froze. No one moved. Within a couple of minutes, it was pitch black again. I looked back and saw Scotty on my side of the trench. It was time to move. Sergeant Stevens hand-signaled us to move in a single file, keeping close to the ground, almost hunched over—our weapons in one hand, the other on the ground. We weren't running, but we were moving at a brisk pace to the breach in the wire where we would pass through it."

As I listened to Patrick's recounting of World War I, I felt as if I were there. Pauline didn't move as he was talking, but I could see she was ready to leap in to reassure him at any time.

"It only took a few minutes to reach the breach. The order in which we exited the trench was the same as the order in which we went through. The opening was very narrow, and we had to crawl through it. No one wanted to expose their entire body. It was just wide enough for one of us to pass through at a time. I looked at my watch, and we were on time. In all my life, I had never been so aware of time as I was that night."

As he talked about his watch, it was the first time I noticed he was wearing one. His rolled sleeve unrolled as he spoke. As he spoke and gestured with his hand, his arm rose, revealing a wristwatch that I hadn't noticed before.

I asked, "Patrick, is that the same watch on your wrist? Does it still run?"

He replied, "It is." He brought it up to his eyes as if he were about to tell me the time. "No, no, it doesn't. I haven't heard it make a sound since the exact time I was blinded. I don't know why I continue to wear it, but I do. I think it means to me that when time stopped, but my life didn't." He rolled his sleeve back up and continued.

"Once we got to the breach in the wire. I took up an overwatch position as Willy, Rusty, and Lar made it through. I heard machine gun fire in the distance—far enough away not to worry. The three had taken up positions and would keep an eye on me as I moved.

Then Sergeant Stevens and Scotty went through. It only took a couple of minutes to get us all through the opening. It felt strange being on the other side, with just the six of us. In front of us lay two German armies, but we didn't have time to dwell on that. Sergeant Stevens gave Willy the hand signal to move along the bank and toward the boat waiting for us. I was so glad it was pitch black. Doing this mission with clear skies and a full moon would have been a suicide mission."

He paused, and as he did, I could see that he was getting restless. I hoped he wouldn't just get up and bolt. His eyes were closed, but I could see them moving back and forth. He was there in France, fifty years ago, as he spoke. He was seeing it all over again. He reached for his glass, and Pauline handed it to him. He then took a long drink, almost emptying his glass. Pauline asked him, "Patrick, do you want me to fill up your glass?"

He replied, "No, I'm good, thank you."

My mouth was as dry as if I were going down a trench. I didn't realize I was so thirsty as I picked up my glass and took a drink.

After a short pause, he continued, "We moved along the bank toward our boat in a single file at a pretty good pace. All of a sudden, Willy stopped and motioned for the Sergeant to move to his position. Everyone froze. I didn't know what was going on. We all got in the prone position. I could see Willy pointing down to the opposite side of the river. I looked in the direction he was pointing and saw why he stopped. On the other side of the river, a German patrol was moving toward our intended exit point after the crossing. The clouds that had been providing good cover began to clear. The German soldiers on the opposite bank became very visible in the little illumination the moon provided.

Now, I have never smoked, but it seems those who do will smoke at any time and anywhere. Well, one of the German soldiers lit a cigarette as he walked. I heard the sound of a shot from a rifle while I watched in disbelief. The soldier who was smoking fell to the ground. One of our snipers had taken a kill shot, and he was down. The other Germans fell on their bellies and started to return fire in the direction from which the deadly rifle shot had come. We didn't move. After a couple of minutes, I turned my attention back to Sergeant Stevens, who was moving back into his position behind me. As he passed, he put his arm out, signaling to me that we were about to move out. He stopped and whispered to me, 'We are going to slow down and let them move ahead of us. That should give us enough distance between them and us.' I looked at him, nodded, and started to move, but much more slowly.

As we continued to move, I lost sight of the German patrol. I looked back and didn't see any other patrols moving down their side of the river. While we were moving, all I could think about was whether the sniper's unit knew we were crossing the river. To say the least, it weighed on me. I later learned that there was a thirty-yard-wide stretch that was a safe zone for us to cross. If we had been out of that zone, hell, who knows? Lucky Rusty was excellent at land navigation. He honed his skills in the forests of France, so dense that without a map and compass, one would undoubtedly get lost.

It only took us fifteen minutes to reach the boat. We paused before it, and Willy and Rusty went ahead to do a quick recon and check for booby traps. Willy remained at the boat for security, while Rusty returned toward us, paused briefly, and gestured for us to proceed."

# CHAPTER 10

CROSSING THE MARNE

As the afternoon wore on, sitting on the porch became increasingly uncomfortable due to the heat. The breeze was nearly nonexistent, yet Pauline and Patrick appeared very comfortable. I suppose spending time in an air-conditioned office has made me soft, but I wasn't going to admit it to them. I removed my sports coat, draped it over the back of the chair, took my handkerchief from my front shirt pocket, wiped my forehead, and took a gulp of my lemonade.

"Gordon, do you want to go inside?" Pauline asked. "You look like you're burning up."

I wanted to say, "*Yes, yes. Can we go in?*" But I replied, "If you guys want to, sure, I'm good."

She responded, "Once the sun goes behind those trees across the street, it will be fine. Let me get you some more lemonade."

I handed her my glass. She took it and walked into the house.

I touched Patrick on the knee. He almost jumped out of his chair. I guess his mind was on the banks of the Marne River. I said, "Sorry, Patrick. Is everything okay? I didn't mean to startle you."

Laughing, he replied, "No. I always jump up when someone touches me. Hell yes, you startled me, but you're good, Gordon."

Pauline walked out of the house as he said, 'Hell yes.' "What's going on, you two?" Pauline asked. We both started laughing. She mumbled, "Boys will be boys."

She placed my full glass on the table, sat back down, and said, "Gordon, here is a wet towel."

As she handed me the towel, I rubbed my face. Then put it at the base of my neck. It felt so good. The cold water was refreshing. We both waited for Patrick to continue his story.

"At precisely 2355, we started to feel the rumble and hear the thunder of our artillery. It wouldn't be long before we saw the smoke screen. We had only a few minutes to get into the boat and cross the river.

As we moved down to the boat after getting the all-clear from Willy and Rusty, I looked left and right along the river and saw a couple of hastily built wooden footbridges the Germans had constructed. Only one was fully intact, and that one might be our way back across the river to friendly lines. The others were out of commission. Our engineers did a great job rendering them inoperable. While the Marne's current is relatively slow, a lot of debris floats down it. Therefore, we had to be cautious as we crossed the river to avoid any obstacles. We didn't want a piece of wood to pierce our boat. Neither I nor the others wanted to swim or wade across it. As the rest of us moved along the bank, I saw our boat was between two tree stumps under a tarp. With Willy and Rusty providing security, Sergeant Stevens motioned for Lar and me to remove the tarp covering the boat. Scotty took up a position behind the boat to push it in once we all got in."

I interrupted and asked, "Patrick, there was one guy who could push the boat in with all you guys in it?"

Patrick started to laugh. "Scotty was a big guy from New York City. I don't mean overweight; he was at least six feet three and must have weighed at least 250 pounds. Heck, I think he could have pulled us across the river. Lar and I slowly pulled the tarp off so we could put it in the boat. As we pulled it back, we looked inside the boat to ensure there were no booby traps. Once the tarp was off, I placed it in the boat. I then got in and looked for the paddles. There were five lying on the floor.

I called Sergeant Stevens over and said, 'There should be six. One for each of us rowing and one to steer.'

He replied, 'We will have to make do.' He motioned for Rusty and Willy to come over to the boat.

We all grabbed hold and moved the bow to the edge of the bank, barely into the water. Rusty and Willy jumped in the boat and picked up a paddle. Rusty sat in the front on the left side, and Willy was opposite him. Lar was next to get in. He took the next paddle and sat behind Willy. Sergeant Stevens followed him, took the last paddle, and went to the back of the boat to steer it. I got in and took up a position at the front of the boat to look out. I had my rifle at the ready. Sergeant Stevens gave the hand signal for Scotty to start pushing the boat.

With it already partially submerged, it was little effort for him. Once the boat was entirely in the water, he handed the BAR to Sergeant Stevens as he jumped. As he attempted to climb in, he lost his footing and fell into the water. As he struggled to get in, Sergeant Stevens extended his arm. I was sure the noise he was making in the water would give the Germans away that something was going on in the river. Scotty tried to grab his hand as he was about to get in, but a tree stump crashed into him, hitting him on his side and breaking the grip between them. The sound of him struggling to get into the boat was gone. The Germans never heard him. Our artillery drowned out his attempt to get into the boat. The weight of his gear and the current dragged him to the bottom. I looked back but didn't see him. No one said a word. We just paddled across the river."

"Patrick, was his body ever recovered?" I asked.

He shrugged his shoulders and replied, "I don't know. With the river's current, I don't know how far he could have been carried or whether he got lodged in debris. He was a good man and a fine soldier. He would give you the shirt off his back."

Patrick leaned forward, took a deep breath, and then continued, "Since Scotty was gone, Sergeant Stevens gave me the BAR. We were about halfway across the river, which was only about sixty-five yards wide, and my feet were getting wet. The boat was leaking like a sieve. I took off my helmet and started to bail out the water. The closer we got to the bank, the lower the boat rode in the water. The more water we took on, the longer it took to reach the bank. I thought for sure the mission was about to be over before it had even begun.

Suddenly, Sergeant Stevens took his helmet off and started bailing too. At least, with his help, we were able to maintain the water level in the boat. Rusty turned his head and said, 'Hold on!'

Just then, I saw a log coming toward the side of the boat, looking like it was going to be a direct hit on the side of the boat, surely knocking us over. It didn't knock us over, but it did knock us off course by at least twenty yards by the time we regained control. Sergeant Stevens had to stop bailing and return to being the rudder. I continued bailing, but at a faster pace.

Right on queue, our artillery support stopped the barrage, and we started to paddle a little faster. I knew for sure I would be exhausted by the time we reached the bank, if we did. The guys started rowing faster and faster. We all wanted to escape from this death trap.

After Sergeant Stevens started steering the boat again, we were only ten yards from our intended exit point. After another ten minutes or so, I looked up and saw we were only a few feet from the bank. I stopped bailing, grabbed my gear, and waited until we hit land.

Once we hit it, holding the BAR in one hand, I was out of the boat. I grabbed the rope tied to the front of the boat and tied it around a big rock. It wouldn't be long before the boat was submerged. After that, I moved forward a few feet and provided security. No one moved for a couple of minutes. We wanted to make sure the Germans didn't see or hear us. I don't know what we would have done, but we would have died on that bank if they had. However, we wouldn't have given up without putting up a fight.

The bank we landed on was about fifteen feet tall and sloped at about thirty degrees. I climbed up the bank and took a quick look. I didn't see any Germans, so I gave the hand signal for the rest of the squad to move to my position. I may not have seen any Germans, but I saw the ravages of war from my position and with the bit of illumination from the moon. I could see a small village to my front. It looked like someone had taken a sledgehammer to it. Even in the darkness, the destruction was unbelievable. I thought, *How are the citizens of this town going to rebuild?* It didn't look possible. Everyone got out of the boat and lay to the left and right. Sergeant Stevens was next to me, to my left. Remember, I said I thought I would be exhausted. I wasn't. My adrenaline was flowing, but I wondered how long it would last.

Rusty took out his map and pointed to the location of the command post. Sergeant Stevens looked at the map and pointed to our left, which was our signal to move out. We were aligned in the same order, minus Scotty. I carried the BAR."

# CHAPTER 11

ENEMY TERRITORY

Both Pauline and I listened intently as he narrated his story. The level of detail was exceptional for a man of his age and for an experience that occurred fifty years ago.

He had been speaking for over an hour by then, and I asked, "Patrick, do you want to take a break?"

He replied, "We didn't take breaks in the war. No, I'm going to continue. As we lay on the banks of the river, I glanced down at my watch; it was 0025. We had another five minutes to wait for our contact's signal. I looked over at Sergeant Stevens. His face was expressionless, and he seemed to be somewhere else. As the minutes passed, he continued to gaze into the distance. I nudged him and raised one finger. He looked at me for a moment, then nodded and lifted his finger.

The last minute felt like an hour. Then 0030 passed, and still no signal. 0031, 0032, 0033, 0034, 0035—there was still no signal. In the mission briefing, we never discussed how long to wait if the contact didn't show up or whether to continue the mission or abort. A flaw in the briefing, leaving out a key piece of information.

Sergeant Stevens gave the signal to back down off the berm. Once we had backed down, we huddled, and he said, 'Looks like he is not showing up. We have the location of the German CP and where we should set up our OP. We can make it on our own, but my only question is, do we go without him, and why was it so vital we linked up with him?' No one said anything. He pulled out his map and said, 'We are here. It's another nine miles or so to the German CP. The only thing between us is this town, another one here, a forest, and an open field here and here,' pointing on his map. 'We have to go through this one, but we can skim along the edge of the other one.'

I said, 'Let's get through this one and figure out our next route.' He replied, 'So you guys want to complete the mission?' One by one, we nodded."

I interrupted and asked, "Patrick, why did you guys want to continue without your guide? Weren't you concerned about why he was needed in the first place?"

He replied, "Great questions. I suppose we had hoped he would allow us to move faster. Perhaps he had a shortcut, knew of obstacles, or the placement of German forces. Just to name a few.

Now, why did we continue? There were a couple of reasons. One, we made it that far. Two, we couldn't go back across the river. We didn't know what would happen if we returned too early. That was never brought up in the briefing; we didn't know the signal for aborting the mission. Would it be the signal to our forces that it would be the same if we returned before the pickup time? Again, another flaw in the briefing. We didn't want any friendly fire. Hell, they could have thought, they're way too early; it must be the Germans. So, we decided to complete the mission."

Smiling, he said, "Most of all, none of us wanted to get back in that boat."

I wasn't sure how to respond or what to say. The faith they had in Sergeant Stevens as a leader and in each other was commendable and unwavering, even after losing one of the patrol members so early on in the mission.

"Sergeant Stevens motioned for me and Lar to move back to the top of the berm to get a view and see if there were any Germans or the person we were supposed to meet.

We made it up the berm and scouted around. He was not there, and we didn't see any Germans. I gave him the hand signal to move up. The rest of the patrol joined us. Once we were all there, Willy went over the berm, and we all followed in a single file. Keeping low but moving fast, it was twenty yards to a hollowed-out building next to what was left of a church. As I ran past it, what amazed me was that the stained-glass window of Jesus was untouched. It was as if it had just been installed, with no signs of the war. It was beautiful. When I saw it, I felt a sense of calm. The top of the steeple was gone. What a pity. It once appeared to be a beautiful church before the war. We hustled over to the corner of the building.

Willy peeked around the corner. Rusty was behind him with his rifle at the ready. Sergeant Stevens motioned for me to move up and cover Willy and Rusty as they moved to the next building. At that moment, I felt we would never make it through that area. When I looked around the corner, I saw street after street of blown-out build-ings everywhere. In the daylight, it would have been challenging to navigate the streets. But at night, in almost pitch-dark conditions, it looked impossible. I doubt anyone lived there. If they did, I couldn't see how they could have survived. I knelt, put the BAR up to my shoulder, scanning left and right as I covered Willy and Rusty as they ran across the street littered with bricks, concrete, wooden beams, glass, and metal. As they reached the other side of the street, they were next to the building. The clouds started to break, providing some illumination. When I looked down the street to my right, I saw a German patrol advancing toward us. There were only three of them. I notified Sergeant Stevens by tapping him on the shoulder, holding up three fingers, and pointing down the street. He nodded his head in acknowledgment.

Rusty looked at me from across the street, and I pointed to the patrol. He gave me a thumbs-up when he saw them. Luckily, they were in a position where the Germans couldn't see them. However, they were heading straight to us. The patrol continued to walk toward us, fifteen yards, ten yards, five yards. I put my BAR down and pulled my trench knife from its sheath. Put my fingers through the knuckle guard and held it tightly in my right hand. Sergeant Stevens and Lar did the same. I raised three fingers, indicating that I would take the last soldier in the patrol. Sergeant would take the middle soldier and Lar the first one. My heart was beating out of my chest. I was hoping they wouldn't hear it. I thought it was beating so hard it could be heard."

My heart was pounding as Patrick continued his story. I looked over to Pauline, and her hand was on her chest.

I whispered, "Are you okay?"

She nodded, yes.

"Suddenly I heard, 'Kommen Sie zurück, Korporal.'" The patrol stopped just feet from us. I heard one of the soldiers say, 'Ich wünschte, sie würden sich entscheiden. Sind gleich da.' Crazy, I still remember that. It's ingrained in my brain. I had no idea what he or the other German yelling at him said, but they turned around and walked away. That is when I noticed that sweat was rolling down my face. I glanced back at Sergeant Stevens and Lar and started to laugh. Their faces were covered in sweat like mine. I knew then we were all in this together. I released my grip on the knife. Then, I placed it back in its sheaths. Sergeant Stevens and Lar did the same."

As Patrick spoke about holding his trench knife. His right hand gripped the chair's arm. I could see his fingers turning white. He was holding it so tight.

I stopped Patrick and asked, "Do you want to know what the Germans said?"

He turned his face in my direction and replied, "You speak German?"

"Yep. Someone told them to come back, and one soldier said, "I wish they would make up their mind," and, "We will be right there."

"Well, I'm glad they turned around. Killing with the trench knife is brutal. All we needed was for one of them to scream. Our mission and lives would have been over. Pauline, can I have a fresh glass of your amazing lemonade?"

She picked up his glass with one hand and the pitcher of lemonade with the other and poured him a glass. Once the glass was filled, she placed it on the table. Patrick, upon hearing it being put on the table, picked it up and took a long drink. He set it down, cleared his throat, and continued his story.

"We knelt and waited for the signal from Rusty to move across the street one by one. I saw the signal and tapped Sergeant Stevens on his shoulder. He stood up and started running across the street. When he was halfway across, I got up, looked down the street, and ran across. Lar followed once I was across. As he ran across the street, he tripped and fell to the ground. He lay there for a minute. We weren't sure if he was hurt or wanted to make sure the Germans didn't hear him fall. We got our answer pretty fast. He held up his thumb, giving us the signal that he was alright. He then got up and ran toward us.

He made it across the street. As he stood next to me, I started to laugh. I thought back to when I saw Pauline at the church dance and tripped on my shoestrings. He looked at me and said, 'What is so funny? I guess you have never tripped.' I patted him on his back and replied, 'Have I got a story for you. When we get back, I'll tell ya."

After a short pause, Patrick continued.

"Once we were all assembled, we regrouped and began moving through the debris-filled streets, ensuring we stayed on the side where we would be in the dark in case the clouds opened up, and we cast a shadow.

Sergeant Stevens pointed between two buildings and said, 'Once we get through that alley, there will be a small field and then a forest. We are going to cross the field and get into the tree line. Patty, you will cover us till we get in the field. Once we're all set, Lar will cover you. We will regroup in the field, cross it, and advance into the wood-line. I don't plan on stopping. We are going to move fast. Get down and get ready.' I acknowledged and moved to get a view down the street toward the field.

I took up a vantage point and covered them as they moved into the field. Once they were all there, keeping low, I moved into the field and rejoined them.

Once we all assembled in the field, we moved toward our next objective, the forest. It took at least fifteen minutes to move to the edge of the field.

We stopped, and Sergeant Stevens said, 'Same order as last time. Get ready to move.'

As before, I covered them as they moved into the treeline and followed once I got the signal to move. Sweat was pouring off my face.

We moved five yards into the forest. Even though we didn't know what it would hold for us, we were all tired, hungry, and thirsty. I loved being an infantryman. I looked down at my watch. We had to be in position in four hours, before dawn. We waited near the edge of the forest for Sergeant Stevens to give the order and direction of travel."

# CHAPTER 12



REFLECTION

I looked down at my watch. I couldn't believe I had already been at Patrick and Pauline's house for over four hours. It's almost two o'clock. I turned to Pauline and said, "I can't believe it's almost two."

She replied, "Really, no wonder I'm getting hungry." We all laughed.

She got up and said, "How about I make us a little snack. I'm sure Patrick is getting hungry, and he needs to let his voice rest."

I wasn't going to say anything, but I could hear in his voice that it was getting raspy. While Pauline and I were talking, Patrick just sat there and looked like he was focused on something in the distance.

As Pauline walked into the house, she said, "Gordon, you're staying for dinner, aren't you?"

I could tell by the way she asked the question; it was not really a question but more of a command.

Before I could answer, Patrick said, "Yes, he is staying. Who do you think will turn the crank on the ice cream maker? Not me this time."

"Great idea, Patrick, vanilla ice cream will go great with the apple pie I baked this morning."

I hadn't had homemade ice cream or apple pie in years. There was no way I was going to turn down their offer for a home-made dinner and ice cream.

I got up and went over to Patrick, put my hand on his shoulder, and said, "I'll turn the crank, but you can't eat any till after dinner."

He started to laugh and replied, "I'll do it myself."

There was something about Patrick and Pauline. I couldn't put my finger on it, but it was special. They were a perfect match, both independent, but they relied on one another. I remembered back to what she said to him at the train station when he got back: *'You listen to me, Patrick Wayne King. I see the man I fell in love with. I see the man who fought for his country, and now I see the man I'm going to marry. So, never ever again tell me you're not the same man. Whatever the future brings, we will do it together.'*

I sat and reflected on Patrick's story. He unfolded in front of Pauline and me. I thought back to my father and what World War I was like for him, and how he died. However, I would never know, as any letters or information about him were burned in our house fire in the early 1930s. I had my birth certificate, but it had my stepdad as my father and no mention of my real father's name. Maybe it was for the better. My stepdad provided an excellent life for my mom and me. He treated me like one of his children. I'm going to let sleeping dogs lie.

As I sat there, Patrick took off his hat and wiped his brow without saying a word. I was focused on Patrick until I heard Pauline walking out of the house, so I got up and opened the screen door. She was carrying a plate of homemade peanut butter fudge and a pitcher of cold milk. My mouth started to water when I saw the plate of fudge. I thought, *my favorite.*

As we sat there, eating fudge and drinking the most delicious cold milk I had ever tasted, I asked Patrick, "While you were in recovery, what did you think you were going to miss the most with being blind?"

He sat there for a minute, then answered, "Well, I have to put them in two buckets. One bucket is civilian life, and the other is military life."

I found his reply to be most interesting.

He said, "Civilian life, there are so many, and it's complicated, of course, seeing Pauline, my mom, and dad. Now, the military is much easier. One is being a part of something, a team. I was afraid I would lose that feeling. I never had it before I joined the Army. I loved the camaraderie within my unit. Everyone was looking out for one another. Back then, I knew I would feel distant from my Army buddies and the isolation that came with being blind."

I interrupted and asked, "Patrick, have you ever had a reunion for the unit?"

He put his right index finger to his temple, slid it down with his middle finger under his nose, and replied, "Interesting enough, yes. There have been a couple, but I only attended the one in '38. That was our twenty-year reunion. Since most of the guys lived on the East Coast, Pauline and I traveled there by train. The first train I had been on since I got home. That stirred up a lot of emotions, but we made it. It was great to be around the guys. We toasted to the friends we lost and to a better future for our children. The isolation I dreaded was nonexistent. I felt secure. I was back in the Army. I love those guys."

Patrick got up, told Sarge to stay, and walked into his house to resume playing the piano. This time, the music was upbeat and joyous.

Smiling Pauline leaned over to me and said, "That was a great question. Thank you."

# CHAPTER 13

INTO THE FOREST

After a few minutes, Patrick emerged from the house after playing the piano. As he walked past Pauline, he touched her shoulder, bent over, and kissed her on the cheek.

She looked up at him and asked, "What was that for?"

He answered, "No reason, I didn't want to miss the opportunity to kiss you."

I'm not sure if I have ever seen a more profound love between two people. Now, my mom and dad were in love, but Pauline and Patrick were different.

She didn't say anything, just sat there and smiled.

Patrick sat back down, took a drink from his milk, coughed, and continued his story.

"As we waited for the orders from Sergeant Stevens to move deeper in the forest, we kept a lookout for any Germans.

We knelt there in the tree line. Lar tapped Sergeant Stevens on the shoulder and asked, 'Do you hear them?' Not waiting for a response, he said, 'The Germans were where we just came from,' as he pointed in the direction of the voices. 'They just came from that area we were just in.' Sergeant Stevens tapped Willy and Rusty on their backs and gave the hand signal to move to the left down the treeline. Once they got in position, he was followed by Lar, then me.

As I entered deeper into the forest, I looked back and saw the shadows of the German soldiers as the clouds parted. I rushed back to the tree line, turned around to face the Germans, and took up a prone position as I got situated. I felt a tap on my shoulder. I looked around, and we were moving. Sergeant Stevens wanted to put as much distance as possible between the Germans and us. If the Germans came in our direction, there was going to be a fight. We continued through the forest and got close enough to see a group of mobile artillery pieces with crates of shells. They must be storing them out of sight for their next offensive. I looked to the left and moved toward where there were at least 10 additional artillery pieces. I knew then that the Germans were coming exactly where we were. They were the crew of the cannons we just passed."

* * *

"It was pitch black in that forest. After all the years of fighting, there were still forests and fields that had escaped the ravages of war. This was one of them. It was slow going as we moved. Every few yards, we would stop to listen and ensure we were heading in the right direction. It would have been very easy to get turned around and lost in the forest during the day. At night, it was almost assured. It was a slow go navigating through the woods. We were all exhausted, hungry, and thirsty by now.

After about one hundred yards or so, we stopped, and Sergeant Stevens said, 'Circle around me.' In front of him was his map. He took a twig that was next to him, pulled out his flashlight, and said, 'Lar, cup your hands around the light. I don't want the Germans to see it.' He put his hands around where the light was coming from. With the twig, he pointed and said, 'We are here.'

He then took out his pocket notebook and recorded the artillery's grid coordinates and other relevant information. He also jotted down the location where Rusty went into the river. We weren't only on a mission to cut the communication lines going into the German Command Post, but also on a reconnaissance mission. Every key piece of intelligence Sergeant Stevens added to his notebook was invaluable."

I interrupted and asked, "Patrick, why didn't he just use his finger?"

"Ha, Gordon. Great question." He held up one finger. I could have sworn he was seeing his finger. Then he said, "Hold up one finger. Look at it. See how wide it is? When you put it on a map, it might cover five hundred yards. Depending on the map, that's a considerable distance. Using the twig, you can pinpoint the locations."

I pulled my head back. It was as if I had just learned the world was round. It made so much sense. I should have known that. But flying at 300 miles per hour, hundreds or thousands of feet off the ground, I only needed a general location. I said, "Well, Patrick, I learn something new every day."

He just smiled and replied, "That's a good thing. You're going to learn a lot today."

I didn't even second-guess him. His statement was profound. Today would be a day of learning about World War I and each other.

He continued, "He pointed to our location on the map and the route we would follow to the objective and said that it would take at least two hours to get there. Depending on how quickly we could move through the woods and whether we encountered any more Germans.

Sergeant Stevens motioned for Lar and me to go over to him. He said, 'I want you to take ten minutes and scout around here and see if there are any additional artillery pieces or military equipment.' He looked down at his watch and held up all of his fingers. Indicating we had ten minutes.

Lar and I set out on our scouting mission. It only took a couple of minutes before we could see more artillery and a few machine guns still in their crates. We took a few more minutes to look around, then made our way back to the patrol.

I leaned into Sergeant Stevens and said, 'There were at least ten additional artillery cannons and some crated machine guns where we just scouted.'

He took the twig, pointed to a location on his map, and asked, 'Here?'

I nodded.

He then asked, 'What direction were they facing, and were they in a line?'

I replied, 'Yes, in a single line and pointed to the southwest toward our lines.'

He took out his compass and shot an azimuth in the direction the artillery was pointed. He then took his pen out of his pocket and marked the map. He patted Lar and me on the back and said, 'Great job, both of you.'

He looked at each of us and said, 'We need to speed up the pace a tad.' We all nodded. He held up two fingers. Meaning we had two minutes till we moved out.

He then held up one finger. That would give us enough time to quench our thirst, and that was about it. Luckily, we each brought two water canteens. As I finished drinking, I heard, 'Let's move out.' I looked at my watch. It would be getting light in a couple of hours, and we still had a few miles left."

Patrick stopped and shifted in his chair, looking uneasy. He put his hands on the chair arms and pulled himself up, almost sitting straight up.

* * *

"Well, we were moving pretty fast and making good time. Willy was the pointman and at least ten yards in front of us. Suddenly, there was a loud bang and a brilliant flash of light. We were moving so fast, we didn't even look for booby traps. The next thing I heard was Willy's screams, then they stopped. Silence. He set off a booby trap, and I moved to where he was. I was very confident that there were no booby traps along the route he walked. So, I moved very fast, running toward him. As I got up there, I got on both of my knees and put my ear down to his face. I didn't hear him breathing or feel any air from his mouth. I checked for a pulse. There was none. I looked down. He was missing both his legs. Everything from his waist down was gone. It wouldn't have mattered if he were next to a hospital when he tripped the mine. There was nothing anyone could do. He had set off a mine."

Patrick's voice started to tremble when he spoke.

"There was nothing I or anyone could do. As I knelt there, Sergeant Stevens said, 'Grab him and pull him into the trees over there, slowly. There might be more booby traps.'

I grabbed what was left of him by his utility straps with one hand. I dragged him by his harness and laid him in the trees. With my free hand, I felt for more booby traps. I was in a very dense part of the forest. I stopped, put my hand in his jacket, and felt for the cord that secured his identification disks. I pulled on the cord, and it broke. I took both identification disks. I would give one to Sergeant Stevens and leave the other in his jacket pocket. I did a quick prayer and left him there among the trees. We were now worried about the Germans coming to see what had happened.

Before we left, I grabbed his rifle and ammo, trench knife, and hand grenades. Sergeant Stevens distributed the ammo and put the rifle over his shoulder. He then took his map out and marked the location on it where Willy was killed. I could see in Sergeant Stevens' face that he knew we would have to find another route back to our rally point to meet up with the infantry squad. But right now, he had one mission. Get to the objective and complete the mission. We were two men down. I looked around before we left our fallen friend. There was no way they would find him before daybreak. I hid him pretty well."

Patrick dropped his head down and wiped tears from his eyes. Pauline got up and hugged him. I sat there and started thinking of my dad. *Is that how he was killed?* I wish I had known him.

I could hear Pauline ask him, "Do you want to stop? I think

Gordon has all he needs for the article," as she looked at me. I nodded and replied, "Yes, I have enough."

He picked his head up and said rather sharply, "No, no. I'm not done. There is so much more to tell."

Pauline put the palm of her hand on his face and wiped the last tear away with her thumb.

"As we continued to move through the forest, there weren't any additional booby traps. I'm guessing it was left behind. It must have been there a long time and was never cleared. In the distance, we could hear the Germans moving very quickly to where Willy was killed. After five minutes, we could see the forest clearing. But there was no time to stop. We were nearing our objective."

# CHAPTER 14



PATRICK'S DIARY

As the sun started to shine directly on the west side of the porch, Pauline got up and put her arm around Patrick. She looked at me and asked, "Gordon, can you please move our chairs over here so we can get out of the direct sun? We already have one there, so bring two, please."

I replied, 'Of course."

I picked up Patrick and Pauline's chairs and put them on the back porch. Once I put the chairs down on the back porch, I went back and grabbed the lemonade.

Once we were all seated, Patrick resumed his story.

"It was almost sunrise. I could see the sun rising above the horizon. With the drifting clouds, it was beautiful, an orange glow on the horizon, and darker as I looked up. The only thing that disturbed what otherwise would have been a perfect morning was the sound of artillery from the direction we had just maneuvered through. As we got closer to the edge of the woodline, we started to crawl. Luckily, we didn't encounter any more booby traps. When we got to the edge of the treeline, there was a field of green grass as far as you could see.

We weren't sure what was on the other side of the open field we were about to move through. I had to do a double-take. Even in the dark of night, the field looked so peaceful. I thought my mind was playing tricks on me.

Lar nudged me and whispered, 'Do you see what I see?' I replied What? 'How peaceful it looks,' he said. I shook my head in agreement.

I just smiled. My mind was in another place. I closed my eyes for just a minute and saw Pauline and me lying on a checkered blanket, looking at the sky, enjoying a picnic."

As he spoke, a big smile came over Patrick's face. He looked at peace.

"Well, my solitude didn't last long. I heard, 'Come on, we're moving out.'

Sergeant Stevens did a quick look at his map and pointed down the woodline, then said, 'We are going to skirt the treeline for a while longer.'

We got up and moved back ten yards into the treeline, then continued to our objective. Keeping eyes on where we just came from, where we were going, and the open field to our left.

After thirty minutes, we stopped. Sergeant Stevens took out his binoculars. It was now light, and the battlefield was in full view. I looked to my right, and no more than ten feet away were four crosses with German helmets on them. They were graves. I got a bad feeling in my stomach. These couldn't be the only ones, and if there were dead Germans, there had to be live Germans in the area. I motioned to Sergeant Stevens, and he looked over, acknowledging them. He gave the hand signal to close in on him.

Once there, he said, 'Okay, guys. Where we are going to set up for the day is that little building on this side of the hill.' He pointed to it and its location on the map. Patrick and Lar, I want you to recon this building to make sure it's empty. After our contact failed to show up last night, I don't have much faith in the intelligence the briefer provided us about that building. You two will check it out before we all move in. I want to use it as our OP on the objective. Move along the treeline, then stay on the backside of the ridge. It should take approximately thirty minutes.'

Looking at his map, he said, 'But if you need more time, take it. Take your time, we have it. Once there, signal me by waving your arms from that back slit in the wall. Do you see it?'

I acknowledged.

He continued, 'I want to ensure that whoever we are supposed to link up with is not fighting for both sides, and we don't fall into a trap.' Once I get the all-clear, Rusty and I will take the same route you took and meet you there. We will set up an observation post, eat some chow, and rest. Get ready to leave in thirty minutes. I want to wait and see if any Germans are moving out there.'

Both Lar and I acknowledged.

"With the time we had. I decided to take out my diary and write a little bit."

I stopped Patrick and asked, "You had a diary?"

He replied, "Yes, we all got one. Some folks wrote in them, but most didn't. No, I didn't have one. I still have one! Pauline, can you please go get it?"

Patrick didn't notice that Pauline was already in the house, retrieving his diary. She was already back on the porch by the time he finished asking her to get it.

"Patrick, I already went and got it. Here, Gordon." She handed me his diary, and I said, "Mind if I open it up and read a couple of your entries?"

They both replied in unison, "Of course not. Read them out loud."

I opened it about halfway and started to read some of the entries.

* * *

*"May 23rd, 1918. We have completed all our training and are preparing to relocate to another location to join the rest of the unit. Everyone is in high spirits and ready to get into the fight. My buddy Lar and I had ammo detail yesterday. I don't know how many boxes of ammo we moved, but it was a lot.*

* * *

*June 10, 1918. The rain was coming down today. It started last night and has not let up since, well into the day. The roads are muddy, and the vehicles are struggling to move troops and equipment. However, the weather isn't preventing the Germans from continuing their constant shelling."*

* * *

I stopped reading and said to Patrick, "These entries are an excellent record of the war from a soldier's perspective."

He replied," Yes, and no two are alike. Everyone wrote from their field of view. But we didn't share them. They are very personal."

"Can I read some more?" I asked.

Patrick nodded.

* * *

*"June 16th, 1918. As we began moving to the front, it was an endless stream of soldiers and equipment. Soldiers from France, England, and, of course, the U.S. I have never seen this many people moving in one direction."*

* * *

*June 25th, 1918. The weather has been nice the last few days. We moved up to the front near the Marne River. This is a place that has seen its fair share of war. If the Germans attack, it will be their second attempt. Lar and I were tasked with helping to dig out the new Company Command Post during the last artillery barrage. It was damaged. It only took us a couple of hours. After that, we just sat around and took turns looking over the trench into No Man's Land. I miss and love you, Pauline."*

* * *

I skipped a few pages and read another entry.

* * *

*July 8th, 1918. Wow, it's hot—over 90 degrees. All I do is sweat in my uniform. Something is up. There is a lot of activity at the front. There is considerable movement, and the artillery has been consistent, employing both high explosives and gas. I hate gas. I had guard duty at the CP, and there was a lot of activity, with soldiers coming and going—more than usual. I wrote you a letter. I hope you get it. If not, this is my proof that I wrote one. Love you. "*

* * *

*"July 9th, 1918. The Germans are intensifying their attacks and shelling. Soldiers are dying all around me. There are so many, not just one at a time, but in clusters. We try to get some distance between each other, but in the trenches, it's hard. Not much room, so when a trench takes a direct hit, it's death and destruction. Death is not just from shrapnel but from gas, too. When I feel the wind blowing in the direction of the Germans, I know it might be a good day or at least a brief period without the threat of gas. Along with the artillery attacks, the Germans have unleashed their Stormtroops to conduct surprise attacks, killing many soldiers. Everyone is on edge. By the way, I got put in a new squad after an artillery attack."*

* * *

I went to the last entry and started to read.

*"July 10th, 1918. Taking a short rest, I thought I would write a little bit. Out on a patrol and lying here in a forest.........."*

* * *

Patrick blurted out, "I never got to finish the entry. We had to move out. It was time for Lar and me to recon the OP. That was my last entry, and it was also the last time I wrote in it."

I closed the diary and handed it back to Pauline. She took it and clutched it against her chest. It would have taken a pry bar to get it from her.

I thought to myself, *Did my father have one? Did he write in it? If so, where is it?*

I said, "Patrick, please continue. Sorry for interrupting.

# CHAPTER 15

OBSERVATION POST

Sitting in the shade felt good. The fudge and milk were holding me over until dinner, which I couldn't wait for. I felt right at home with Patrick and Pauline. Since the war, I usually feel uncomfortable around strangers, but they didn't feel like strangers. I think that is what I like about being a reporter. I understand the story and move on without needing to get to know the person I was interviewing. I talk and meet a lot of folks, but I spend very little time with them. Perhaps I will return to my old self and become more outgoing and extroverted. One could hope.

Without skipping a beat, Patrick started again, "Those thirty minutes passed in a flash. I was so drawn to writing in my diary and getting ready.

At five minutes till, Lar crawled over and asked, 'Well, are you ready, Patty?'

I looked over and nodded. We got up and walked over to Sergeant Stevens.

When we got there, he tossed me his binoculars and said, 'Stay within the woodline and take your time. We don't know if there are any more booby traps. I have kept an eye out and haven't seen or heard any Germans. Give me the BAR, it will slow you down, and it will allow me to provide cover fire just in case.'

I put the binoculars around my neck and handed him the BAR with the ammo pouches. I felt naked without it. He gave me Scotty's rifle and ammo. I took another look at my map and made sure I had my compass with me. I shot an azimuth toward where we were headed, then Lar and I headed out. He was in the front, and I was behind him. As we moved along the woodline, the forest became increasingly dense. I couldn't believe that after years of war, it looked like it hadn't been touched. Fortunately, it provided the best cover and concealment we could have asked for. The bad news is that it did the same for the Germans, so we moved with purpose but cautiously.

After about fifteen minutes, I tapped Lar on his back and pointed to the field. I low-crawled to the edge of the woods and looked through the binoculars, then quickly checked my map and compass to ensure we were heading in the right direction. It would have been so easy to get lost. That added weight to my shoulders of land navigation made me double-check everything."

"Patrick," said Pauline.

"Yes, dear," he replied.

"What is low-crawl and an azimuth?"

"Sorry, Pauline. Low crawl is when you get on your belly and move along the ground like a snake. Here, let me show you." Patrick got up, and Pauline replied, "Oh no, you won't. I just washed your pants and shirt."

By this time, Patrick was laughing out loud. I started to laugh too.

"What's so funny. You two?" inquired Pauline.

"Honey, there is no way I'm going to low-crawl. Those days are gone."

She walked over to him and nudged him, laughing. She bent over to me and whispered, "It's a good day."

"I heard that, and yes, it is," yelled Patrick.

"Hey, what about an azimuth? I still don't know what that is."

Patrick was the first one to speak up. "It's simply a degree in direction. There are 360 degrees in a circle. Think of true north as 360 degrees and south as 180 degrees. We use an azimuth for movement. Let's say we are moving in an azimuth of 90 degrees for 200 yards, which means we are moving east for 200 yards."

Pauline nodded and said, "Okay, I'm good for now."

She leaned into me and said, "I think I will ask for directions."

When I started interviewing Patrick, I thought it would be another interview. It turned out to be a day I would never forget, and with two people who brought out emotions in me that I had suppressed for years. I didn't know if I was ready.

"We made our way to the edge of the treeline, and I took out my binoculars. I had a perfect view of the small concrete building that was to become our OP. The field in front of us would provide excellent cover as we move to the OP. The grass was tall and moved in the light breeze. I thought that at any time, a horse-drawn mower would appear and cut the grass in front of us.

I tapped Lar on the shoulder and gave him the arm signal to start moving to the OP. He led, and I was right behind him. I looked at my watch. As Sergeant Stevens said, it should take only about 30 minutes to reach it. As we approached it, our movements would be cautious and deliberate. Every fifteen yards or so, we would stop and listen. I would take a quick peek over the tall grass when we reached the front of the building. The side facing out lines.

On that side, there was a small slit, not large enough to crawl through, but it provided a great field of view for the German soldiers to observe our movements across the front lines. He both got down on one knee, rifles at the ready. We stayed that way for a couple of minutes to ensure we weren't detected when we arrived at the OP. After a few minutes, I motioned to Lar that I was going to take a look inside through the slit in the wall. I stood and slowly looked in. I couldn't see inside the entire building, but it looked empty.

The only way in was through the front door opening. There was no door on it, and it faced the Germans. I had a bad feeling about that place. We would have been sitting ducks if they had caught sight of us. I motioned for Lar to take the left side and for me to take the right.

Staying as low as possible, I put my back against the outer wall as I move very slowly to the side. With each step, I was careful not to make any noise. I stopped about halfway, put my ear up to the wall to listen for any movement in the building. Although I looked into it, I suppose I was being overly cautious or paranoid. I didn't hear anything, so I continued to the front. As I got closer, I lowered myself to the ground. I wanted to be the smallest target possible.

When I reached the edge of the building, I noticed that the grass in the field had not been cut, so it would provide cover to move into the building, just like the other field. However, I did notice a path through it leading to the building. It had been used, and not too long ago. As I looked to my left, I saw that Lar was lying prone. I pointed to the front entrance. He got up on one knee, then started to duck-walk to the entrance. When he arrived, I followed suit. When we were both there, I entered first with my rifle at the ready. Lar was right behind me.

Once we got in, I went to the slit in the wall and waved for Sergeant Stevens to move to the building. He acknowledged and went into the treeline. I looked at my watch. Thirty minutes until he and Rusty would arrive. It was going to be a long thirty minutes. I kept an eye out for Sergeant Stevens and Rusty from the front door.

Those thirty minutes were the longest thirty minutes as I looked out of the door to my left. I looked at my watch. Thirty-one minutes had passed. Suddenly, I saw someone crawling around the corner of the building. With my knife at the ready, I motioned to Lar. I put my two fingers to my eyes, then moved them to where I was looking. Hoping it was Sergeant Stevens or Rusty.

After a few seconds, I saw it was Sergeant Stevens. I put my knife back in its sheath. He entered first, followed by Rusty. I shook their hands as they entered the building. I was relieved we were all together again."

Patrick sat there without saying a word.

Pauline got up and said, "I'm going to make dinner. You boys stay out here and enjoy the beautiful Arkansas summer day. I have something for you two to do."

I couldn't believe it was almost dinner time. The peanut butter fudge did a great job holding me over till it was time to eat. Patrick and I sat there; you could have heard a pin drop. I didn't want to interrupt what he was thinking.

Suddenly, Pauline walked out of the back door carrying an ice cream maker. She placed it on the porch and said, "Gordon, come with me. You can bring out the salt and ice."

I got up and followed her in. She pointed to the ice and salt. I picked them up and carried them out to the porch. I looked around, and there she was, holding a metal cylinder. It looked like it had just come out of the refrigerator. With the humidity, steam was coming off it.

She took the crank off the ice cream maker, inserted the cylinder with the ice cream mix, put the crank back on, and secured it with a fastener. Then she said, "Gordon, pour some ice around the cylinder, then pour some salt. Repeat until it's about here," as she pointed at a point in the wooden ice cream mixer. When I was done, she said, "Now turn the crank till the ice cream mixture gets the consistency of ice cream."

"Hey, hold on, I can check to see if it's ready," Patrick said, holding up a finger.

Laughing, Pauline said, "Let me get you a spoon. Where were you born in a barn? Where are your manners?"

"Pauline, you know I was born in a barn."

I smelled into the cylinder and said, "Wow, that smells great. What's in there?"

She replied, "Half and half, heavy cream, sugar, and vanilla extract."

I smiled and started to turn the crank.

# CHAPTER 16

THE SKIES OVER FRANCE

Patrick and I sat on the porch as I started churning the ice cream in the ice cream maker. Pauline opened the screen door and asked, "Gordon, how does fried chicken, collard greens, and potatoes sound?"

I couldn't get the reply out fast enough, "Yes, ma'am."

She closed the door, and I started to churn. After a few minutes, my mind raced back to October 1944, the skies over France. The churning of the ice cream maker reminded me of opening the cockpit canopy of my P-38 over the skies of France in October 1944. I noticed that I was sweating and had stopped cranking.

Patrick noticed when I stopped, and he said, "Gordon, the ice cream can't be done yet. Why did you stop churning?"

I started churning again, and I said, "Patrick, remember when you asked me why I stopped flying for American Airlines?"

"Yes," he replied.

"I...One day, I had a flashback, and the co-pilot had to take control of the plane. That was the first one I had had in years, and it was the most intense. After that incident, I knew I couldn't fly anymore. I didn't want the responsibility of having the lives of everyone on another plane. So, I resigned, and when I got home, I told my wife. She didn't understand or comprehend what I was going through. Our marriage didn't last long after that. Once we broke up, I decided to get a job where I was only responsible for myself and no one else. That was five years ago. Since then, I haven't spoken to my son more than a couple of times. I wouldn't even call what we talked about a conversation. I didn't want him to see that his dad was broken."

In a raised voice, Patrick said, "Hold on, Gordon. You are not broken. Why would you say that? Hell, if you're broken, I must be Humpty Dumpty. I'll never get put back together again. So, what happened? I'm here to listen and not judge."

"I guess the cranking of the ice cream maker took me back to October 1944 over France. It was like I was sitting in my plane and cranking the canopy open of my P-38. The flight I was on conducted a strafing mission against a German anti-aircraft gun battery in the open. It looked like an easy target. We were coming back from providing support to a B-17 bombing mission over the central part of Schweinfurt, Germany.

I was the last plane in the formation and went in for the kill. As I pulled up on the yoke, I felt rounds impact my aircraft, and I saw smoke coming from the right engine, which had taken a direct hit from the flak, knocking it out. I pulled the yoke to gain some altitude. But my plane was not responding to my movements and controls. I had to add altitude if I wanted to jump out. I was too close to the ground to survive. I then noticed I was hit. Blood was everywhere in the cockpit. I wasn't even sure where I was hit.

I started to lose consciousness, and the plane began to dive when I heard, 'Son, wake up. You have to get out of your plane.'"

"Gordon, someone was talking to you. Who was it? One of the other planes in your flight?" Patrick asked.

I shook my head and said, "No, my coms were out. I couldn't talk to anyone.

Well, the loss of blood was inducing shock, and I thought I was dreaming or dying. Sweat was pouring down my face. Hearing the voice, I wiped the sweat from his face, opened my eyes, and tried to pull back on the yoke again to gain altitude. I couldn't bail out. I was still too close to the ground. I would never have survived the jump. My chute would never fully open. The plane was not responding to my control corrections. I took my hands off the yoke and resigned to die.

As I went in and out of consciousness, I could hear the left engine start to sputter, sputter, and die. I lost both engines and all power, and I knew the plane would stall. Suddenly, the plane began to gain altitude, 100, 200, 300, and 400 feet. I rubbed my eyes and looked at the altimeter. I couldn't understand how the plane was gaining altitude with both engines out. There was no way the plane was defying physics. I shook my head and glanced down again. The altimeter read 1000 feet, and with all my might and senses, I cranked the handle and then pulled the lever to open the canopy. It wouldn't budge. I didn't have the strength to open it.

Then I heard, 'Try again, son. Try again. Son, son, now! Don't die here as I did.' I tried again."

I looked at Patrick, and he didn't make a sound. He was listening to my every word.

"I put my hand on the lever and pulled. The canopy flew off. I looked down at my leg, where I got hit. It had stopped bleeding, but fire was starting to engulf the cockpit. I unbuckled my harness and attempted to exit the aircraft, using my legs and all my remaining strength to support myself. I blacked out. I woke and felt lighter than air. Somehow, I got out of my plane—the force of the air and its coldness woke me up. I looked up and saw that my parachute was fully deployed. I looked to my right as my plane hit the ground and exploded. I knew then if I survived, I would be a prisoner of war. I blacked out again.

I woke up only feet from the ground. I braced myself for the impact on the ground. I hoped I would remember what I was taught in fighter school. Bend your knees and let yourself go. I looked to the right and left and saw dust plumes from vehicles approaching from two directions. The ground rushed up, and as I hit the ground, it caused a new pain in my right ankle, but the worst pain was from my burnt skin. I forgot all about the shrapnel in my leg. I couldn't even remember how I caught fire, but the wind from jumping from the plane put out the flames. When I hit the ground, I pulled my .45 caliber pistol from its holster. The pain was excruciating. I blacked out. The last thing I saw was someone running toward me. I didn't know if it was the Germans or who.

Now, after bailing out of my plane. I have a different attitude toward the soldiers who jumped on D-Day and today's paratroopers. They are a different breed.

So, lying in a field, I woke to someone grabbing me. I opened my eyes and saw it wasn't a German soldier. It was a woman. I said, 'Je suis américain.'

She replied, 'Yes, I know. We saw your plane get hit and watched you bail out. We are here to get you out of here before the Germans come. I'm with the French Resistance. Now listen, where are you wounded?' She asked.

I pointed to my leg and ankle. Mumbling, I said, 'My back is burned pretty bad.'

She looked at my leg. The bleeding had stopped. 'Okay, you're not bleeding, and well, your ankle is broken. I don't want to mess with your back.'

While she was tending to me, two other members of the French Resistance ran up and said, 'Come on, Camille. The Germans are coming.'

She replied, 'Take him. I will cover and meet you over there, pointing to the tree line.'

'Camille, please let me stay here,' her friend pleaded.

'No, you and Henri are the only ones who can carry him. My arm hurts.'

Her friend, Henri, looked at her and said, 'You're hit.'

'The other man hesitated, then replied, 'Henri, we need to get out of here. The Germans are coming. Now grab under his right arm. I will hold his left side.'

'Hey, he has a leg wound, his ankle is broken, and he has some severe burns on his back. Now go.' She started firing at the Germans who were running toward us.

I thanked her and said, 'God be with you,' as they picked me up and ran to their car. As we drove off, I could hear the German machine gun fire and Camille returning fire. Then I could only hear the Germans firing.

Camille died in that field in Germany rescuing me. It's my fault she is dead. Why did I live and not her?"

"Gordon, you didn't cause her death. She died fighting for her country. She knew in her heart that by saving you, she might be saving France. Why did you live? It was God's will. It wasn't your time. It sounds like you have survivor's guilt," Patrick said.

I sat there for a bit and took in what he said.

"Yes, maybe I do. I never thought of that. Patrick, do you think it was my dead father talking to me? After all, he did die in France. Telling me to get out and giving me the strength to open the cockpit? I never really pondered it, but maybe he was my guardian angel."

He didn't say anything for a couple of minutes. I looked over to him, and he was in deep thought. Suddenly, he said, "Yes, I believe things like that can happen. I don't know how or why, but they do."

"Has anything like that ever happened to you?" I asked. Before he could answer, Pauline stood at the screen door and asked, "Is the ice cream done?"

I looked down and replied, "Yes, ma'am, it is." I didn't even realize I was turning the crank the entire time Patrick and I were talking.

She replied, "Good, now go wash up. Dinner is ready. Gordon, please hand me the ice maker, and I will put the ice cream in the freezer. So, how much did Patrick eat already?"

I looked at Patrick, and he was smiling. He replied, "Not one spoon, not a one."

"Like I believe you. Show me the spoon," she smirked.

Patrick held it up and said, "Clean as a whistle."

We all laughed.

I felt better after telling Patrick what happened in France and how I thought I was the reason for Camille's death. Everyone knew I was shot down, but not about Camille, and the guilt I felt for her death, or the voice of my dad, which I heard. I held it in for so long, it was tearing me apart inside. Up until that time, Patrick was the only person I ever told the entire story to. I knew it was safe with him. I felt a sense of relief.

*American Marines digging trenches, Lucy-le-Bocage, France, 1 June 1918. (Alamy)*

*American soldiers in trenches, France, 1918. (Alamy)*

*1917, 369th Infantry African-American Regiment (Harlem Hellfighters. (Alamy)*

*U.S. soldiers putting on their Gas masks, 1918, Northern France. (Alamy)*

*U.S. Soldiers defending a fence line, in a shallow trench, Northern France, 1918. (Shutterstock)*

*Leave no man behind. U.S. Soldier retrieving the body of a fellow soldier in No Man's Land. Northern France, 1918. (Shutterstock)*

*Meuse-Argonne American Cemetery, Romagne-sous-Montfaucon, France, June 2024. (Travis Davis)*

*Author with Wife after folding the U.S. Flag at Meuse-Argonne American Cemetery, Romagne-sous-Montfaucon, France, June 2024. (Travis Davis)*

*Author's Wife's Great Grandfather (Uropa), 1916 German Soldier, Coburg, Germany. Before moving to the Western Front. (Martina Davis)*

*American 155 mm artillery cooperating with the 29th Div. in position on road just taken from the Germans. A Battery 324th Artillery, 158th Brigade in France / Signal Corps. (Library of Congress)*

*U.S. Marines Digging Trenches in Northern France. (Library of Congress)*

*Members of the Three Hundred and Fourteenth Ammunition Train receiving mail. St. Baussant, Meurthe et Moselle, France. (Library of Congress and American Red Cross)*

# CHAPTER 17



Patrick and I went into the house. Right behind Patrick was Sarge, never leaving his side. He walked over to the sink and washed his face and hands. Pauline pointed toward the bathroom. I went in and did the same. The cold water on my face felt good.

I walked back to their kitchen. Pauline was still standing by the gas stove, tending to a black cast-iron skillet. The smell of the food she was making made my mouth water. I haven't had a home-cooked meal in years. I seldom cooked; I always ate out, at McDonald's, or at some other fast-food joint.

They didn't have a formal dining area. The dining table was in the kitchen, against the back wall. There were only two chairs around it. Pauline motioned for me to grab a chair from the living room and place it around the table.

I grabbed the chair and put it across from Patrick. I offered to help Pauline, but she insisted that I sit down. Sweet Tea was already on the table. First came the potatoes, then the collard greens, followed by fried chicken, and finally some homemade white bread with butter.

We all sat down and held hands as Patrick said a prayer, "Oh lord, thank you for this excellent meal, as we welcome our new friend Gordon into our house. Please guide and protect us as we navigate our way through life. Please give us the strength to overcome any challenges. Keep us safe on our journeys wherever they may take us, and wrap your hands around our fallen comrades. Amen!"

Pauline looked over at me and said, "Gordon, you look different. I can't put my finger on it, but something is different. "Relaxed. That's what is different. You look at peace."

I nodded.

Pauline handed me the plate of chicken. "Take what you want, Gordon, you just have to eat what you take."

I picked up a chicken leg. She put a chicken breast on Patrick's plate. She then placed a forkful of collard greens on his plate, followed by some potatoes.

I watched as she carefully placed the food on his plate.

She said, "I put the chicken at twelve, the collard greens at six, the buttered bread at three, and the potatoes at nine." He said, "Thank you, and Pauline, it smells delicious."

I finished piling my plate up, and as she was putting food on her plate, she asked, "So what did you guys talk about while I was in the kitchen?"

I had just taken a bite from the chicken when she asked the question. I put my finger up to indicate hold on for a minute. Once I chewed and swallowed the chicken. I wiped the crumbs from the breading off my face. I replied, "Wow, Pauline. This chicken is amazing."

I sat there for a bit and said, "I told Patrick about when I was shot down in France during World War II."

"What, you were shot down! Are you okay?" Pauline blurted out.

I replied, "Yes, I was burned and had a leg wound, and when I hit the ground, I broke my ankle."

"Hit the ground in your airplane?"

"No, I jumped out. With a parachute, of course. But the landing was still hard."

I decided then that I didn't want to hold anything back from

Pauline, and I began to tell her the entire story, just as I had done with Patrick. She sat there without making a sound. I don't even think she touched her food the whole time I was talking. At one point, she got up and hugged me.

When I was done, she said, "So, how did you get back to America?"

"Once the French Resistance put me in their car, they took me to a small farmhouse. There, they cared for my wounds and put a brace on my ankle as best they could. The burns weren't as bad as they thought; they dressed the burns and then took care of the shrapnel from the anti-aircraft gun. I was extremely fortunate.

They knew the Germans would be looking for me, and if they found me, would turn me over to the Gestapo, so after a few hours, they moved me to another farmhouse and handed me off to two other resistance fighters. Jean and Sophie were a married couple fighting the Germans. Their job was to get me to Allied Forces. If I had been shot down a few months before, they would have taken me to Spain.

The French Resistance had underground railroads. Similar to the efforts during our Civil War to help slaves achieve freedom. I couldn't move fast, so we waited a few days, hoping the Germans would look elsewhere. At that time, U.S. and allied forces were already in France and moving toward Germany. However, pockets of loyal German soldiers and a sympathetic French population remained loyal to the Germans.

On the fourth evening, while we were sitting in the farmhouse having dinner. Sophie took out the two-way radio and sent a message asking where they could take me. The reply came back within a minute. She jotted it down, turned around, and smiled. She walked over to Jean, and he looked at the note and started to laugh.

They both spoke pretty good English, so I asked, 'What is so funny?'

He handed me the note, but I couldn't read it. It was in French.

Before I could ask what it said, Sophie turned and read it, 'They are coming for you. They want us to hold up here. An Army unit will be here in the morning to pick you up and get you to a hospital. When they get here, a lieutenant will say, 'I have a soldier with a broken ankle. Can you help him?' Our reply is 'We have one too.'

* * *

The next morning, a platoon from the 442nd Regimental Combat Team arrived at the crack of dawn, picked me up, and took me to the rear. I must say that when the lieutenant walked in, I was taken aback. He was Japanese, but I didn't care. I just wanted to get home. The medic with them did a quick once-over.

He asked if I could walk, and I replied, 'Yes.' I was going to walk out of there. I thanked Jean and Sophie for hiding and taking care of me. I walked outside, took a deep breath of the fresh air, and climbed into the jeep for the ride to the field hospital.

* * *

Once I was cleared for travel, I checked out of the hospital, and I boarded a ship back to England. I stayed in the hospital for a few weeks.

When my ankle and wound were healed, and my back was on the mend, one of the new flight surgeons examined me and cleared me for flight status again. However, if I wanted to fly, I would have to ship to the Pacific. There was an unwritten rule that if a pilot who was shot down was aided by the French Resistance, they didn't want that pilot to fly again in Europe, just in case they were shot down and captured by the Germans. Those pilots were known to get tortured until they broke.

I wanted to fly again. So, I volunteered to be assigned to the Pacific Theater. They flew P-38s in the Pacific, and I just loved flying them. They were a tad squirrelly but a lot of fun to fly. When I got there, I was assigned to the 49th Fighter Group. I only flew a few missions before the war ended. Once the war ended, I came home, and well, you know the rest."

I didn't even realize that when I stopped talking, my plate was clean. I was eating the entire time; it was as if I had never eaten before.

Pauline said, "Gordon, that was some story. I think you need some warm apple pie and vanilla ice cream. What do you think?"

I replied to Pauline, "Well, I'm pretty full, but I think I have an empty spot right here," pointing to one side of my stomach.

Patrick chirped in, "Hey, what about me?"

Pauline got up and walked over to Patrick, put her hands around his face, kissed him, and said, "Yes, of course."

# CHAPTER 18

TIME FOR APPLE PIE AND ICE CREAM

Pauline started to clear the dinner table. I got up and started helping her clean up. "No, no, Gordon. You are our guest," Pauline said.

I replied, "I'm sorry, Pauline, but I always helped my mom clean up the table, and I'm not going to start not helping now."

"I think your mom and I would have gotten along."

I put the dishes in the sink, hugged her, and replied, "Yes, you would have been two peas in a pod."

Even though my mom died many years ago, I still miss her, and helping in the kitchen that day brought back good memories. As I was standing in front of the sink, filling it up with hot water and putting in some dish soap, I heard Patrick get up and the sound of Sarge's claws along the linoleum floor. I felt a hand on my shoulder.

Patrick said, "Now you're doing my job." There was no way I would get in the way of Patrick doing the dishes. I asked Pauline, "What can I do?

She answered, "Why don't you get some plates for the pie and ice cream. They are over in the cabinet." She pointed to her left.

I walked over, took out three plates, and put them on the table.

Pauline turned and said, "Oh, no, we're eating outside. It's too beautiful an evening."

As they stood by the sink, Patrick washed the dishes, and Pauline dried them. I sat at the table and reflected on the day's events. I never in a million years could have conceived our conversations. From learning about Patrick's World War I story and sharing my story with both him and Pauline about my years-long battle and guilt over the French woman's death, Camille, all those years ago. I felt at peace. Somehow, I knew there was more that Patrick had to tell. What I didn't realize at the time was the impact it had on me.

"Patrick, why don't you and Gordon take those plates from the table to the front porch. I'll get the ice cream and pie and meet you out there."

As Patrick and I sat down, he asked, "Gordon, are you okay?" I didn't expect you to tell your story to Pauline, but I was not going to stop you."

"You know what, Patrick, I'm good. Very good, it felt good."

He put his hand out, and I grabbed it, saying, "Thank you."

Sarge got up, walked over to me, put his paw on my leg, and barked. "Gordon, there are some snacks over on the window ledge. I think he wants one. He likes you."

I got up and walked over to the window ledge to get a snack. I turned around, and Sarge was eagerly waiting for his snack. I held out my hand, and he took it with so much care and lay down next to Patrick.

Pauline came out of the house with a tray in her hand. On the tray was a piece of pie for each of us, along with a container of ice cream, forks, and spoons. She set it down on the small table, handing one plate to Patrick, one to me, and taking the other.

I took a bite of the apple pie with a little ice cream and said, "Hmm, this apple pie is delicious, and the vanilla ice cream is a perfect match." I put my fork on the plate and said, "Pauline, this is the best apple pie I have ever had."

She replied, "Well, get ya another piece. There is plenty. Now, if you want more ice cream, you'd better get it before Patrick eats it all."

Chuckling, Patrick said, "I do love ice cream. Another scoop, please."

Between spoonfuls of ice cream, Patrick continued telling his story, "I was manning the front door, and Lar was watching out the slit in the back wall. Sergeant Stevens and Rusty were sitting down along the right side of the wall and trying to get some rest. The sun was shining through the clouds, and the temperature was rising. There was very little wind, and that small building held the heat.

Suddenly, I heard trucks moving in front of us. I stood up to get a better look and see in which direction they were heading. Sergeant Stevens had already gotten up and was on the other side of the door.

He asked, 'What direction are they heading, and how many?'

I replied, 'It looks like they are moving southeast toward the river, and there are four. I couldn't see if there were any soldiers in the beds of the trucks. Each one was covered.'

He took out his notepad, and as he did, a letter fell out. He quickly picked it up and put it back in his jacket pocket. I wanted to ask him who it was from, but he would have told me if he wanted me to know. He looked at his watch and jotted down the time, the direction of travel, and the number of vehicles in the column. The column of trucks drove off into the distance. I kept watch on them till they disappeared.

Sergeant Stevens moved back to the rear of the building. He tapped Rusty on the shoulder and motioned for him to follow him. After a couple of minutes, they approached the door.

Sergeant Stevens said, 'Rusty and I are going to scout to see if we can find communication lines. If so, we will mark them and return at night to cut them. Once we do that, we will return to the pickup point. Since we need to take an alternative route, I have been exploring a few options.' He pointed out the route on his map.

He continued the briefing, 'It appears that it will take us an additional hour. So, we will be out of here at seven at the latest. It won't be completely dark, but we can't wait any longer. It's going to be tricky. We should be back here in a couple of hours. Let's sync our watches. I have 1420. If we are not back here by 1620, move back into the woods here.' He pointed to a spot on his map. 'Take cover, then at 1900 move to the pickup point. Use the route that gives you the best chance of returning safely. I think the one I showed is the best, but again, use your judgment.'

I took out my map and marked the route he discussed.

He handed me this notebook and said, 'Give it back to me when we return. In the event we don't make it back here. Make sure the CO gets it!'

I replied, 'Roger,' and put it in my pocket.

Sergeant Stevens and Rusty exited the building and set out on their recon mission.

Lar and I stayed back in the building and kept looking out for the Germans."

I put my plate down after two pieces of pie and three scoops of ice cream. I asked Patrick, "While they were gone, did you and Lar discuss the route back in case they didn't return?"

Pauline got up and put another scoop of ice cream on his plate as he was about to speak. He took a spoonful, savoring it. Then took another.

He put his plate down and replied, "I had the route he suggested on my map. We didn't at first, but after an hour and a half, we started to discuss what we would do. Should we wait a little longer or retreat into the woods to the rally point? I looked at my watch, and it was 1625. The two-hour time limit had passed. As we were about to leave, I noticed some movement to our front. I put my rifle to my shoulder, finger on the trigger, took a deep breath, and waited to identify what was moving. I pointed in the direction I noticed the movement to Lar.

He scanned the area and was ready when suddenly I heard, 'Patty.' I knew then it was Sergeant Stevens and Rusty. They both entered the building. Both were covered in mud. He looked at his watch and said, 'You two should have been gone by now. Next time, adhere to my orders.' We both nodded.

Both of them went to the back of the building. He motioned for me to join them there. 'We found two communication lines and marked them,' as he pointed to his map. He continued, 'You and I will take this wire, and Lar and Rusty the other. It will take about thirty minutes to reach them. Once the lines are cut, both teams will move to the rally point in the woodline. Give me a few minutes, and I will provide the timeline for completing this mission.'

I went back to the door and briefed Lar."

"Patrick, you guys had already been in the building for a few hours. I would think you would want to get out of there." I asked.

"Well, you are one hundred percent right, but we had daylight to deal with. So, we knew we had maybe a couple more hours. We were all getting itchy to move back to our contact point and make our way back to friendly lines."

I looked over to Pauline. I saw pride in her eyes. Patrick had never provided her or anyone with much detail about the war. She sat there and admired him. We still hadn't even gotten to when he was blinded. I still wanted to ask about Lar, but it wasn't the time. I'm sure he will get to it. He took the last bit of ice cream, set the plate down, and said, "Gordon, you did a great job."

I leaned back, smiled, and waited for him to continue his story.

# CHAPTER 19

TIME TO LEAVE THE OBSERVATION POST

I could tell Patrick was getting anxious. He started to fiddle with his armchair. Pauline noticed, too, and looked at me. I shrugged my shoulders. She just stared at him, wanting to help, but there was nothing she or I could do. This was up to him. We were there to listen.

Patrick leaned forward and started up again. "At around 1700, Sergeant Stevens and Rusty moved up to the front door where Lar and I were positioned.

He knelt and said, 'First thing, when we cut the communication wires, the ramifications will be immediate; the Germans will retrace the wires to where they are cut. Based on how far their CP is from where we cut them, we have about a ten-minute head start. With that, let's do some backward planning. He put his map on the floor and said, 'It's 1700, we need to be at the link-up point no later than 2400. However, I want to be there thirty minutes early to provide security before they arrive. That means being at the link-up point at 2330. I don't want them running into an ambush. That gives us six and a half hours to cut the communication lines and reach the link-up point from now. Since we know where the lines are, it will only take us at most one hour to reach them, cut them, and link up at the rally point in the woodline. Patty, you're with me, and Lar, you're with Rusty. Okay, is everybody with me?'

We all nodded.

'We need to get some rest, and I don't want to leave too early, so be ready to leave at 1830. We all leave at the same time. We have an hour and a half left here. I don't want the wires cut till 1915. We have to cut them simultaneously. Once we cut the lines, we have a ten-minute window to get as far away as possible, hopefully to the woodline. That is how long I think it will take to trace the wire back to where it was cut. Let's check our equipment, take thirty-minute guard shifts, and try to get some rest. Lar and Patty, we will take over.'

I looked at my watch, then started to check my equipment."

Patrick took off his hat, wiped his brow, put it back on, and leaned back in his chair. He looked uncomfortable.

Pauline asked, "Patrick, are you okay?"

He sat back and replied, "Yes, just getting my thoughts together."

I reviewed the questions I had pre-written, which I had asked every other WWI veteran I had interviewed so far, up to Patrick. They were of no use for the story Patrick was telling me. I put them back in my briefcase.

"It was gosh, I think around 1730, and Lar and I had taken over watching out the front door. In the field to my right, I heard a noise. It wasn't someone walking or running, more like someone struggling to move, very slow, but a lot of noise. I put my arm back to get Sergeant Stevens' attention, then motioned him toward the door. He joined Lar and me. I held up my index finger to my right ear and then pointed to my right. We had been fortunate so far. We only heard the German patrol earlier. Whoever or whatever it was, it was getting closer. In an instant, right in front of me, a German soldier popped out of the tall grass. I looked at him, and he looked at me. Before he could get a word out, I rushed out of the building and put my hand over his mouth. As I was trying to keep him quiet, Lar pushed him to the ground. What was strange to me was that he wasn't struggling, as I would be. I would be fighting for my life if I were him.

'He's bleeding,' whispered Lar.

Then it made sense why he was not struggling. I looked at Sergeant Stevens, and he motioned for me to bring him into the building. I took out my cloth from my front pants pocket and put it in his mouth. All we needed was for him to yell and give away our position. We both dragged him along the ground to the building. Once we got him in, we laid him on his back. There was blood everywhere. Rusty started to provide first aid, but it looked like he was not going to make it. Around his shoulder was a leather pouch. I took it off and started going through it. As I did, the wounded soldier was moving his head from side to side, as if he didn't want me to look inside.

I opened the pouch and pulled a sealed envelope. Written on the sealed envelope was, if I remember correctly, General Max von Boehm."

I stopped Patrick. "Patrick, sorry for interrupting, but how in the world are you remembering all these details. All the vets I have interviewed, so far, not one of them had the memory recollection as you do."

He looked forward. "Gordon, I relive the events every day. Every day, it's like I'm there. I can see every detail clearly in my mind. It was the time before my darkness," he answered.

I shook my head in disbelief.

My interrupting didn't stop Patrick. "I handed the envelope to Sergeant Stevens. He looked at it, then opened it. What I didn't know at the time was that he knew a little German. He opened the envelope and pulled out some papers that were fastened together with bank pins. He turned it toward me. The top paper read, 'Streng geheim. ' I shrugged my shoulders.

He said, 'It says Top Secret.'

As he was looking over the papers, he started to mumble, 'These are battle plans. Written instructions, timelines, troop movement, strengths, and maps. We must get this back. How is he doing?'

Rusty looked up and replied, 'He won't last long. Looks like he has lost a lot of blood. I wonder if he just stumbled here, or if this is a link-up point to transfer the plans to another runner?'

'Well, we might as well get as much information out of him before he is dead.' Sergeant Stevens took the cloth out of his mouth, leaned over him, and said, 'Wie heißen Sie?' The German soldier just looked at him. When he tried to talk, blood would leak out of the side of his mouth. Sergeant Stevens put his ear to the soldier's mouth to better hear him. He said it again, 'Wie heißen Sie?'

I could barely hear his reply, 'Ernst.....Schwämmlein. His voice trailed off.'

Even though he was the enemy, I admired him. He was severely wounded, but he wanted to complete his mission. He made it to the concrete building within visual distance of the German CP.

As Lar was standing by the door, he said, 'Quiet. There is someone out there.' Sergeant Stevens whispered, 'I guess we have the answer to our question. He is here to pass along the information.'

Rusty took out a trench knife and put it to the throat of the wounded soldier. I looked at him and whispered, 'What are you doing? He is still alive.'

He replied, 'Not for long. We can't leave him alive. If the Germans find him and he can somehow communicate, he will give us away.'

I never saw that side of Rusty before. His eyes had hate in them. I know Germans had killed his friends, but they killed mine too, and I'm not a killer. This German was helpless. Suddenly, his body started to lurch up and down, and he was trying to scream 'Amerikanischer Soldat.' I put my hand over his mouth, and Rusty took his knife and thrust it into his chest, killing the German soldier.

Those were his last words. He died right there.

Rusty turned to me and said, 'I told ya.'

Sergeant Stevens reached into his shirt, pulled out his identification tags, removed one, and put it in his pocket.

Suddenly, we heard, 'Schwämmlein!'

We all looked at each other. 'Ich bin hier,' replied Sergeant Stevens.

The other German soldier replied, 'Ernst?'

'Ja, ich bin's, der Ernst. Schnell.'

We moved the German soldier to the right side of the building. Sergeant Stevens and Rusty were on the right side, and Lar and I were on the left. We all had our trench knives out. The first thing I saw was the barrel of the German soldier's rifle; then he walked into the building. He looked at me, dropped his rifle, and started to run out the door. I ran after him and tackled him.

As we struggled, I firmly gripped my trench knife, pushed him down, and then got on top of him, rolling him over. I plunged the entire length of the blade of my trench blade into his chest, pushing it through his back. I pulled it out and plunged it again. His mouth opened, and he took his last breath as I looked into his eyes.

With his last breath, he said, 'Mutti.'

I rolled off of him. My breathing was labored. I thought he had stabbed me. I looked into the sky, and standing over me was Lar.

He looked at the dead German soldier and said, 'You alright? Did he get ya? He's only a kid. They are sending kids to fight.'

I got up and looked at him, then searched for his papers. I found them in his front jacket pocket. I opened them up and saw his name, Hermann Ott, and his birth date, 28.5.1902. He was barely over sixteen. What a shame, but I did what I had to do. He would have given us away. I put his papers back in his jacket pocket.

I dragged the dead soldier into the field and went back into the building.

Sergeant Stevens said, 'We leave in two minutes. The same plan, but we're moving it up; we need to get out of here. Once that runner doesn't show up, they will look everywhere for him. He has battle plans for an upcoming offensive. We need to get out of here. He is already late!'

'Rusty, you and Lar, take him out to the field and try to hide his body. Get ready.'

They carried his body out of the building and about ten feet into the field, and covered him with grass. As they made their way back to the building, Sergeant Stevens and I were already out. He pointed to Lar and Rusty in the direction of the wire to cut. Lar nodded, and both groups split up and went in different directions."

* * *

"As Sergeant Stevens and I were making our way to cut the line, I asked, 'What does mutti mean?'

He replied, 'It's German for mom. Why?'

I answered, 'No reason, just curious.'

He stopped, grabbed me by my jacket, and said, 'You did what you had to do. He was the enemy. If he had had the chance, you would be the one lying in that field, calling out to your mom. Now get it out of your mind, we are in a world of shit right now.'

The look in his eyes said it all. Not scared but determined. He was a great leader."

# CHAPTER 20

CUT AND RUN

As Patrick told the story of Rusty killing the defenseless German soldier, it still bothered him after all these years, or was it his killing the young soldier? Patrick never said. He was very uneasy in his chair. Sarge could sense a change in Patrick's emotions, so much so that he got up and put his head in Patrick's lap. Patrick put both his hands on Sarge and stroked his head. "Patty, do you want to stop for a while. It's getting late?" Asked Pauline.

"What time is it?" he replied.

"It's almost seven."

Patrick replied, "No, it's still early, and it's getting cool. It's nice to be outside. Gordon, if you're up to it. We can continue."

"I'm good. I'm up for it if you guys are."

Both of them nodded. As Patrick continued to pet Sarge, he continued, "Sergeant Stevens and I moved through the field toward where we were going to cut the Germans' communication line. We were about thirty yards from our old OP, and I could hear Germans in the distance, in the proximity of the building. Sergeant Stevens was correct. They are looking for him. If they find the trail of his blood, it will lead them right to the building, from the building to his body, and to the other runner.

'We needed to move a little faster, which was not the easiest with me carrying the BAR. If we moved faster, the probability of our making more noise increased. After ten minutes, I was almost out of breath. I could see that Sergeant Stevens was feeling the same, but we trudged on. He turned, motioned toward the front, and held up ten fingers. Indicating that he would meet me right here in ten minutes. I nodded. He was going to cut the line. I was going to provide a lookout toward the forest to make sure it was clear to move once he was finished. However, I also had to be mindful of the Germans at the outpost we had just left. Lar and Rusty should be in the same position as we are, near the line and about to cut it. I took up a position while Sergeant Stevens cut the line.

I looked at my watch; it was 1810.

I turned toward the woodline, but my mind was on the Germans looking for their soldiers. I watched as he moved deeper into the field. I lost sight of him after a minute or two. I waited for him to return. I put my hand on one of my hand grenades and pulled it off my belt. I put my BAR next to me. I scanned $360^0$ and saw some movement in the direction Sergeant Stevens had left earlier. I looked at my watch; it was 1821. I sure was hoping it was him and not a German."

He stopped petting Sarge. I then noticed Patrick's breathing was getting faster. His head was turning left to right as if looking for something. He was on the move, just as he had been many years ago in France.

"It was him. I put the grenade back on my belt. Sweat was pouring off his face. He put up a thumbs-up. He motioned me to take point and move toward the treeline. After fifteen minutes, we were halfway there when, in the distance, in the direction of Lar and Rusty, I heard the sound of three pops, then a halt, followed by more shots. I didn't want to poke my head up.

I started moving in the direction of the shots, but Sergeant Stevens grabbed me by my leg. I turned, and he said, 'Move toward the woodline.'

As we moved, I heard the distinctive sound of the new Enfield rifles, then the sound of a grenade—boom, then another boom. Rusty and Lar were firing back at the Germans and giving them a good fight. They were still alive and fighting. We were almost to the wood-line when the firing stopped, and the sound of grenades faded. In the distance, I heard the sound of a whistle and the words 'Zwei amerikanische Soldaten, hier drüben.' Then the sound of two shots, I knew they were dead. I prayed for them. I was going to miss Lar, but I didn't have time or the energy to grieve."

The question I had been wanting to ask for some time was just answered. Lar was killed while carrying out the mission and fighting the Germans. Patrick put his head down. Tears were running down his cheeks. Under his breath, I could hear, "I never got to say bye."

He was grieving for his friend after fifty years had passed. Pauline and I sat there, letting him grieve. There was nothing we could say to relieve his pain. He had to let Lar go.

The internal pain he had been carrying along with the death and carnage he witnessed at a young age was something I couldn't comprehend. I had my struggles regarding my war, but they seemed trivial. I know every soldier, airman, marine, and sailor's struggles are their own, and it's not a competition. I knew then I wanted to help other veterans. We need to be there for each other, brothers and sisters in arms. I wasn't always a good listener, a strange thing to say when I'm a reporter. But as I listen to Patrick, I grasp every word and not only the words, but also how he said it, his body movement, and his expressions. It told his entire story. The war was right in front of him as he sat there. His porch became the battlefield.

Pauline got up, hugged him, and asked, "Lar meant a lot to you, didn't he?"

Nodding, he replied, "Yes, like a brother I never had. Let me tell you a quick story. When I arrived at basic training, some of the guys from New York City picked on me because I was from Arkansas, and we talked like we talk. One of the guys must have been six feet three with arms that looked like tree trunks. One day at the chow hall, he decided I needed a kick in the butt. I turned around and hit him with all my might. He just stood there and smiled. Pulled his arm back, and before he could hit me, Lar pushed me down. He took the full force of the punch and didn't flinch. Did I tell ya, he was a steel mill worker? He had been in a few fights and knew how to take a punch. Well, the big guy from New York City started to apologize to Lar.

He stood there and leaned into the big guy and said, 'He is with me. Touch him again, I'm going to……'

The big guy walked off, and Lar shouted, 'By the way, he is from South Pittsburgh. That's why he talks like he does.'

I got myself off the floor and said, 'Hi, I'm Patrick, and thanks, but I could handle him.' He replied, 'I know I didn't want to see any bloodshed, Patty.'

I looked at him, started laughing, and said, 'South Pittsburgh?' We both had a good laugh.

Well, from then on, we were best friends, always looking out for one another. He is one of the people I miss the most."

"Patrick, was Scotty the guy who punched you?"

Laughing, he replied, "Yep. Heck, Scotty turned out to be a good guy."

Without skipping a beat, he continued, "Well, now it was just Sergeant Stevens and me with the lines cut. Well, we didn't know whether Rusty and Lar had been able to cut theirs, but ours was cut. The German whistles were going off in the distance. We had to make it to the woodline, then into the deep forest. That was our only chance at getting back to our lines."

As Patrick spoke, his respiration rate increased. His feet were moving back and forth. I could see that Pauline was getting worried. She was clutching the arms of her chair in a death grip. However, she didn't say a word. He needed to tell his story, and she was going to let him. Yet, the care in her eyes wanted her to stop him and try to get him to relax.

"As we moved into the treeline, it was much different than the night before. During the day, you could see how dense it was, but there were foot trails everywhere. The Germans were no strangers to these woods. I just hoped they weren't in them. Sergeant Stevens pointed to his front. Crouching down, we moved to a small clearing, sat, and waited for the Germans. We could hear them in the distance. It sounded like a platoon-sized group, based on the number of voices and the noise they were making. We got up and moved further into the forest. The further we got into it, the denser it became. I couldn't believe it, after all the years of war, this place was almost pristine. One thing the thick forest did was provide some protection from artillery, or so I thought."

As he said, "Or so I thought," he took off his sunglasses and began to rub his eyes, over and over, as if trying to get something out of them.

"Patrick, stop rubbing your eyes," said Pauline. He put his hands down and looked at his watch. Patrick put his sunglasses back on. Then started up again.

"We continued to move for five minutes or so. The deeper we got in, the sounds of the Germans faded. We moved into some thick brush to take a break. I grabbed one of my canteens and took a long drink. The water tasted so good. It was a hot day, and the lack of water was taking a toll on both of us, but we had to conserve it. We still had a few miles to the link-up point, and within those miles were many Germans searching for their battle plans.

Sergeant Stevens took out his map from his pouch and laid it on the ground. 'Okay, we are here, I think. I want to skirt the treeline, here to here. Once we get to the other side of the forest, we will bypass the village here and move into the field to the pickup point.' As he went over our route, he pointed to each one on his map. 'We might be able to make better time and outflank the Germans. If we are short on time, we will have to go through the village. It will be dark by then.'

The forest was surprisingly quiet. However, I could still hear a lot of activity in the field. They didn't seem to be moving toward the forest. I was hoping they thought by killing Rusty and Lar, they got all the infiltrators."

"Patrick, I hate to ask, but were the remains of Lar and/or Rusty recovered?" I ask him.

He cleared his throat and replied, "I asked a couple of the guys at the reunion, and they indicated yes, and they are buried at Meuse-Argonne American Cemetery. When I found out, I felt relieved."

"How did they find them?"

"I didn't know, but while we were in the treeline in that little clearing. Sergeant Stevens circled on his map where they were killed. He knew where they would cut the communication line, so it had to be around there."

Patrick got up and said, "Sarge, stay." He walked into the house with Pauline right behind him.

I sat there, looked at Sarge, and said, "You're a good boy."

A few minutes later, Pauline opened the door, and out stepped Patrick with Sarge's dinner. Sarge's tail started wagging a mile a minute. He put the bowl on the floor. Sarge didn't move till Patrick said, "Okay, boy, time to eat. Go get it."

He sat back down in his chair and said, "Gordon, when was the last time you talked to your son?"

I was not expecting that question, and I didn't want to answer it. However, I felt compelled to; he had been so honest with me. I took a deep breath and pressed the air out between my lips. "It's been a while, I think at least three years."

"What! Three years," shouted Pauline.

I shook my head in shame.

"Why? Why have you not talked to him? He is your son," said Patrick.

"Great question. I feel I let him and his mother down. I lost a dream job that allowed us to live a very comfortable life. All because I couldn't let the war go on. I didn't want to put him through my pain."

"How old is he now?" Pauline asked.

"Hmm, nineteen."

"I assume since it's summer, he's out of school and at your ex-wife's house. Damn, Gordon. He had to sign up for the draft last year. He might end up in Vietnam. You have to have a relationship with him. You're only adding to your pain. He is old enough to handle whatever you tell him, as I said when you arrived this morning. We have a phone. I think you're underestimating him. If he has to go to

Vietnam, you need to be there for him when he returns. He needs you in his life. You both need each other. Gordon, give him a call. Pauline and I will sit out there and enjoy the evening," said Patrick.

I thought about it for a minute. Then got up and walked inside. I picked up the phone and dialed his mother's number.

It rang twice, then I heard, "Hello, can I help you?"

It took me a second or two to respond. I replied, "Janette, it's me, Gordon. Is Matthew there? I want to talk to him."

"Of course, Gordon, yes, of course. How have you been? Matthew, someone's on the phone wanting to talk to you."

"I'm better, much better. It's time for Matthew and me to talk."

"Here."

"Hello, this is Matthew."

"Matthew, it's Dad."

"Dad? How are you? Are you okay?"

With tears running down my cheek, I replied, "Yes, son, I'm good. I miss you. Do you have a few minutes to talk?"

"Dad, I have all the time in the world. I have missed you." I could tell he was crying.

We spent the next thirty minutes talking. It was as if the weight of the world had been lifted off my shoulders. Just like Patrick said, I had underestimated my son. By the time we finished the call, we had set up a meeting for the weekend in Dallas.

I put the phone down. Wiped my eyes and walked out the front door. No one said a word. I looked at Pauline, then Patrick. Both were smiling ear to ear.

As I stood at the edge of the porch, I said, "Please let me pay for the call." I took a twenty out of my wallet, turned around, and said, "Here, please take it."

Pauline's face got stern, and she said, "No, put your money back. The smile on your face is payment enough."

I looked over at Patrick. He just sat there and smiled. I put the twenty back in my pocket and sat back down.

# CHAPTER 21

DEATH IN THE SKIES

As we sat on the porch, I felt like a new man. Talking to my son after so many years was the therapy I needed. Once we started speaking, it was as if I had just seen him the other day. As Patrick said, I need to be there if my son serves in Vietnam, and I will. There was no way I could repay Pauline and Patrick for encouraging me to call my son. But somehow, I would.

Sarge had finished eating and took his place next to Patrick. Patrick leaned over and started to pet him.

"Once the route was decided, we took off toward the treeline. We kept a deep enough position in the forest to provide concealment, which gave us a perfect field of view as we scanned the area for the Germans. We would switch off being the pointman. After a few minutes, we stopped and listened for any movement ahead or behind us. I heard the sound of a group of airplanes approaching us. I looked up and tried to see if they were one of ours or a group of German planes. Sergeant Stevens moved out toward the field next to the forest to get a better view of the planes.

It only took a minute or two for the planes to come into view. There were six of them, not in any kind of formation. I had to strain my eyes, but I distinguished two of ours and four German ones. Suddenly, I heard the sound of machine guns from the planes firing at one another. The pilots' skill was awe-inspiring. It took my mind off our current situation.

One of the U.S. planes got behind a German plane and unleashed its machine guns. The whine of the engines, along with the sound of machine guns, was a sound I wouldn't forget. They were moving up and down, in an aerial ballet. Each one is trying to get the best position on the other to make the kill shot. They became intertwined in the sky. I saw a German plane behind one of our planes. Then two Germans were behind him. The sound of the machine guns from the German planes (rat-tat-tat) filled the air, and then black smoke started to flow out of our aircraft.

It pitched over and began to fly straight down to the ground. The pilot did not attempt to avoid hitting the ground. He must have already been dead. One of the German planes didn't see our remaining plane lined up behind it and fired a constant stream of bullets into its plane. Black smoke and fire engulfed the plane. I could hear the pilot trying to pull the aircraft up to land rather than crash. However, our pilot had nothing to do with that.

He lined up again and shot a volley of rounds, sending him straight to the ground. I started cheering in my head until I saw two German planes take up position behind our brave flyer. They were so close, I could see the pilot turn his head from side to side to see where the Germans were. He pulled the airplane up, went upside down, did a loop, and got behind one of them and fired his machine guns, knocking him out of the sky. Not to gloat on his kill, he pitched the plane down to hug the ground and tried to outrun the other German planes. But it was no use; they lined up behind him, and both fired their machine guns. Black smoke started to billow from his aircraft. He turned toward us. I looked at Sergeant Stevens.

He said, 'Move now! Get back in the woods. He's coming right at us.'

I could hear the whine of the plane as it got closer as we moved farther and deeper into the trees. We were a few yards deeper in the forest. I could still see the plane. It was low to the ground and coming in fast. Right behind it, but a little higher, were the German planes. Suddenly, it dived to the ground. It didn't crash, but it looked like it landed. The German planes pitched up, turned around to admire their kill. Then flew off into the distance to safety. The brave American pilot and his plane were only ten yards from the forest."

Patrick's breathing became faster and faster, and he began speaking more quickly.

"We both looked at each other. Then back to the plane, with its propeller dug deeply into the ground, and its tail in the air. We just stood there looking at it. Before us was one of our planes, with its pilot still strapped into the cockpit. It wasn't burning, but there was no movement from the pilot. We looked at each other again when I said, 'Should we see if he is still alive?'

I could see the dilemma he was going through. Check on the pilot, who could compromise our mission, or mark the location on his map and the plane's number, and report it when we return to friendly lines. I knew in my heart he would never leave a wounded soldier. We had to ensure he was dead and, if so, notify the higher-ups and his family. It was the least we could do for the brave pilot.

'Damn, damn.' He looked at his watch, then said, 'If we don't hear any planes or German soldiers within the next couple of minutes.'

I thought, *surely the Germans who shot Lar and Rusty would have at least seen the same scene we saw, and if they did, they, too, would make their way to where our plane came down.*

He said, 'I will run out there and see if we can help. If anything, I can take his identification disk.'

I replied, 'Sergeant Stevens, let me go. I think I'm faster than you, and you have the secret message and the map.'

I could hear him mumble something, not quite sure, but it was something about having nothing to go home to.

'Okay, give me the BAR. If you hear anything, get to the ground and come back here. Only check on the pilot to see if he is dead or alive. If he is alive, and you need help getting him out, motion for me to assist. If you can get him out, bring him back here. We will figure out our next move. Understand?'

I replied, 'Roger.'

After a couple of minutes, we didn't hear any planes or ground movement. I handed him the BAR and moved to the edge of the woodline. I looked left and right, then ran into the field. It only took me about twenty-five seconds to get to the crash site. I went to the left side of the plane. That side was facing the forest. I thought it would provide the best cover.

When I reached the plane, I stepped onto its lower wing to get to the pilot. I felt for a pulse, but there was nothing. He was already dead. I unzipped his leather jacket, pulled his white scarf aside, and put my hand in his shirt, feeling for his identification disk. I found them and pulled one off. I pulled my hand out. It was covered in blood. I wiped my hand on my pants, then read it and put it in my pants pocket. I said a quick prayer. I listened for any noise, and in the distance I heard a plane. I didn't think twice. I took off and ran back into the woods.

When I got back to Sergeant Stevens, he said, 'You are pretty fast. Did you get his identification disk?'

I replied, 'Yes,' and handed it to him before putting it into his map bag. He read it and said, 'Rest peacefully, Lieutenant Quentin Roosevelt.' He cocked his head to the side and said, 'Last name sounds familiar.' At that time, the plane I heard sounded as though it was about to land. He handed me back the BAR and said, 'Let's go.' We took off a little deeper in the forest."

"Hold on, Patrick. Do you know who Quentin Roosevelt was?" I asked.

Smiling, he answered, "Well, not at the time. But I found out later. I'll get to that."

I looked at Pauline, and all I could see was pride in her husband. She knew he was a brave man, but never this brave.

She got up, kissed him, and said, "Patty, you never cease to amaze me."

Laughing, he replied, "That's why we have been married for forty-nine years."

I thought, *forty-nine years*. The perfect couple. It would have been so easy for Pauline to move on. She didn't. She would never leave his side, nor he hers.

# CHAPTER 22

A DAY TO REMEMBER

The sun was setting, and I could tell both Pauline and Patrick were getting tired. Heck, I was worn out. I looked at my watch and said, "Wow, it's almost nine. I think we can call it a day. I don't want to take up any more of your time. Patrick and Pauline, I want to thank you for being so hospitable and treating me like part of the family. Patrick, your story is one I will never forget. Thank you for sharing. I will bring a copy of the article before it's published."

Patrick looked in my direction and said, "Hold on, Gordon, I'm not finished. There is so much more to tell."

I replied, "I know, but I can't ask you to keep going. We have been at it all day. I have enough to write the article."

Pauline said, "Gordon, you're right, it's late, and we all are tired. I'll make the guest bed up. You're staying here tonight, and we will continue tomorrow."

"Pauline, I appreciate the offer, but I can go back to Little Rock and come back tomorrow. I don't want to put you both out."

"Gordon, what rank were you in the Army Air Forces?" Patrick asked.

"Captain, when I got out," I replied.

"Well, this is one time a Private is giving you an order. You're staying here tonight, and tomorrow you will have the best breakfast in Arkansas."

I stood up, about to say thank you, but by the time I was upright. Pauline was already walking in the door, saying, "I'll have the bed made in five minutes, and breakfast is at seven. Don't be late." I could hear her chuckling, and so was Patrick.

Smiling, Patrick said, "Gordon, if you haven't figured it out by now. Pauline has grown fond of you, so best not to cross her. There is much more to my story. Please stay, I want to tell you and Pauline."

I sat back down and replied, "Okay, well, breakfast it is, and I won't be late."

* * *

As I lay in bed, I listened to the recording of Patrick's interview. The level of detail he possessed of the events of the war at his age, hell, for any age, was amazing. All the other veterans provided only short stories with some detail, but nothing like Patrick's. As I reflected on the day, a calm overcame me. Not only did I make new friends, but I also heard an incredible story and shared my deepest feelings about the guilt I had been carrying for the last twenty-four years.

But the most gratifying was talking to my son and the promise we made to each other to rebuild our father-son relationship. I felt bad for all these years underestimating my son and his ability to understand my pain. I was in a good place. I was ready for tomorrow. Well, I thought I was!

# CHAPTER 23

ARMY TRAVELS ON A FULL STOMACH

I woke up to the smell of bacon. The aroma filled the house. I looked at my watch; it was six-forty-five. I dozed off listening to the tape from yesterday. After the most restful night of sleep I could remember, I got out of bed, opened my briefcase, and pulled out a toothbrush. It was a habit; I never left home without one. I went into the bathroom, freshened up, got dressed, and walked to the kitchen.

There at the table were Patrick and Sarge. "Good morning, Pauline and Patrick." I walked over to pet Sarge; his tail was wagging.

Pauline was busy making breakfast.

She turned around from the stove and replied, "Well, good morning to you, too. How did you sleep?"

I put my hands on my hips and said, "Like a baby. Best night's rest in years. It's so quiet out here."

Pauline turned back to the stove.

There was another smell coming from the oven. I asked, "Are you making fresh biscuits?"

Without turning around, she replied, "Yes, I sure'em. We thought you were going to sleep through breakfast. Sarge was at the ready to wake you up."

"Oh, I didn't need Sarge waking me up. The smell of the bacon was all it took."

I walked over to the oven, and next to it was a can of Crisco full of lard. I hadn't seen one of those since my mother died. I picked it up and took a whiff. The smell of many cooked meals hung in the air. Not overpowering, but the flavors it brought out when melted were delicious, and what it did for the taste of whatever was cooked with it cannot be described.

"Have you ever seen a can of lard?" Asked Pauline.

I replied, "Oh, yes. My mom had a can next to the stove. But it's been years since I had anything cooked in it."

She took another cast-iron skillet from a cabinet above the stove, poured some of the bacon drippings into it, and began making gravy. The aroma of the biscuits was soon overshadowed by the scent of fresh coffee brewing in their percolator. I almost experienced sensory overload.

"Patrick, can you set the table, please?" Asked Pauline.

He got up and maneuvered around the kitchen as he could see. He went over to the cabinet, took out three plates and three coffee cups, and walked back to the table. He handed one to me and said, "Get ya some fresh coffee, boy."

I replied, "Well, how could I resist? Only if I can get you a cup." He stopped and held out another cup. I took it and filled both of them. I walked back to the table and said, "The coffee is at your twelve o'clock position."

He smiled and replied, "You're a fast learner. Pauline, did you hear what he just said?"

"Yes, Patty."

As the gravy was simmering. She removed the bacon from the other skillet, placed it on a plate, and then started making eggs. Now, she didn't remove any of the grease; she just threw the eggs right in. I could hear the sizzling of the eggs in the hot grease. "I hope you like sunny side up, Gordon?"

"Yes, ma'am, my favorite."

As the eggs were frying. She took the biscuits out of the oven and brought the gravy to the table. Pauline walked over to the refrigerator and took out strawberry jelly and butter. By the time she was finished putting everything on the table. She went back to the stove, put the eggs on a plate along with the bacon.

She sat down, and we prayed.

Patrick said, "Eat up, boy. You're going to need it today." I didn't know what exactly he meant, but I would find out later.

I took a biscuit off the plate, split it in half, and spread some butter on it.

I asked, "Pauline, can you please pass me the jelly?"

"Jelly? It's jam. I made it with fresh strawberries from right here in Bald Knob. Did ya know we are the strawberry capital of the world?"

I replied, "No, I didn't know, and thank you for the jam."

As I put the jam on my biscuit, I took a bite, and I thought I was in heaven. Wow, the homemade biscuit with homemade jam flooded my taste buds with flavor. I then took a piece of bacon along with some eggs. I knew then I was in heaven. I couldn't wait to put some gravy on another biscuit.

"Well, Gordon, how is it?" asked Patrick.

"Honey, don't ask him with his mouth full," replied Pauline.

"Oh, never mind, that answered my question." I almost choked on my food.

After I swallowed my food, I said, "You know it's only a little over an hour drive from Little Rock to here. I could get used to a home-cooked breakfast."

Almost in unison, they replied, "Okay by me."

We must have sat there for almost an hour, mostly eating and a little talking, mainly around how the Razorbacks were doing.

Patrick said, "I may not be able to see them. But I can certainly listen to them on the radio and give them a piece of my mind. Hell, they did terribly last year, finishing 4-5-1. I sure hope they do better this season."

When we were done, I helped Pauline clean up the kitchen while

Patrick fed Sarge. Of course, he got some of the grease. The remaining grease went into the Crisco can.

"Well, ya'll ready to go outside? To enjoy the beautiful morning, and finish my story if I can. One, I'm glad you will be sitting when I tell it," Patrick said.

I didn't want to ask what he meant by the 'if I can.' I went back into the guest room, picked up my writing pad and recorder. I walked out the back door, grabbed one of the chairs, and brought it around to the front. They were already sitting. I put it down and sat. Waiting for Patrick to begin.

# CHAPTER 24



It was a beautiful, yet muggy, July morning as we all sat outside on the porch. The birds were chirping, and a gentle breeze made the leaves on the poplar trees rustle. Very soothing for the soul, but I could see tension on Patrick's face. Pauline grabbed his hand and held it.

Patrick started speaking, "As we got deeper in the woods, the sound of the airplane grew less noticeable. I assumed it landed, and the pilot was checking to make sure the American pilot was dead. I hoped he would overlook that one of his identification disks was missing. Sergeant Stevens said, 'Let's poke our heads out of the woods to see what's going on. I want to see if the Germans had made it to our OP or found their fallen soldiers."

I interrupted, "Patrick, I thought you guys were moving away from the OP and the Germans."

"We did at first, then we backtracked a little bit to see what direction, if any, the German soldiers were moving. We were still a reasonable distance away, and the only way to observe the OP and see if the Germans were moving in our direction was to climb a tree and use binoculars. So, I grabbed the binoculars and set about climbing a tree.

I have to tell ya, I hadn't climbed a tree in years. But some things you don't forget. For a brief minute, I felt like a kid again, climbing a tree in my backyard.

Well, that didn't last long, once I got up to the level I could see. It was not what I was hoping for. The Germans were swarming around the building, and I could see two of them carrying one of their soldiers out of the field. It wouldn't be long before they found the other one. It looked like the runner Rusty killed. I could see they were checking his body. I knew what they were looking for, and we had it. Once they found the other soldier, they would know their battle plans might be compromised. By now, there was a platoon plus of German soldiers. I saw what I assumed was the officer in charge giving orders and pointing to where he wanted his troops to go. Well, I didn't wait for him to point in our direction, so I climbed down and briefed Sergeant Stevens.

He pulled out his map and verified the route he wanted to take. Put it back in this pouch and said, 'Time to move, Patty.'

All we wanted to do now was put as much distance as possible between the Germans and us. With Sergeant Stevens in the lead, we set off. We kept a ten-foot or so distance between each other in case one of us set off a booby trap. By now, we were exhausted, hungry, and thirsty. After half an hour of continuous movement, we made our way to the other side of this forest. There were still two more, or we could go through a village. It was starting to get dark.

Sergeant Stevens stopped at the woodline and motioned me forward. 'We are making good time. So, we are going to rest here till it gets dark. Then move through that village to our right. From there, it's going to be a lot of open land. I don't see another way to make it to the river. Once there, we will hug the bank to the rendezvous spot. We good?' He asked.

I nodded and took out the binoculars and set my sights on that village and waited till dark. I said to Sergeant Stevens, 'Get some rest. I'll take the first watch.' Reluctantly, he agreed.

He hadn't been asleep for ten minutes when a convoy of German trucks drove out of the village. I counted six. A couple of trucks were open in the back and filled with soldiers. The other trucks had tarps covering the beds. They were moving back toward our old OP. I started to wake up Sergeant Stevens when one of the trucks began to sputter, then just stopped right in front of us. The passenger in the cab got out, went to the front, and lifted the hood. I heard him give some commands to the driver. The driver attempted to start the truck, but it was dead in the water.

Sergeant Stevens woke up and said, 'What the hell?'

I replied, 'A convoy of trucks just passed, and one of them broke down right in front of us. That truck broke down,' as I pointed in the direction of the truck.

I continued, 'I'm just glad it's not one filled with soldiers.'

As we were observing the truck. The truck behind him pulled in front, attached a rope, and pulled him off the road in our direction. The driver of the truck that towed him started speaking. When he was done, I asked Sergeant Stevens if he understood what he said.

He nodded and replied, 'Not all of it, but to the effect. Stay with your truck. Corporal Linz will go with us. I will send a crew to fix it. Guard this truck! The driver acknowledged.'

Before we knew it, the rest of the convoy had passed, and the truck and the German soldier were all alone; he was not happy. Yelling and throwing rocks in the direction the other trucks drove off in.'

Sergeant Stevens started to laugh. I looked at him and asked, 'What's so funny?'

He replied, 'The driver is cussing up a storm. He is pissed they left him. I mean, pissed. Says he is going to miss chow.'

After the driver was done yelling. He sat with his back against the front tire in front of us. I said, 'I know it's stupid, but I would love to know what's in the truck.'

With a smile from ear to ear, he replied, 'It's almost dark. I think we can take a look inside. The more information we have to provide the higher-ups, the better.'

I smiled back."

I stopped Patrick and said, "Hold, what about the mission? It seems a bit foolish to risk getting caught. To see what was in the truck."

Patrick replied, "Yep, looking back, it was. But it was worth it. Well worth it. Plus, we decided to go through the village. After seeing all the soldiers in the trucks, we felt pretty good. There weren't many left."

'Okay, now I'm curious,' I said to Sergeant Stevens."

Pauline looked over and squeezed his hand. She said, "You have always been the curious type."

"We crawled out of the forest as the sun went down. It got dark pretty fast. We kept low and to the right flank of the driver, who by now was lying down next to the truck. We kept low, side by side, inching toward the truck. Fifty feet, forty, thirty, twenty, ten, when the driver woke up, and stood with his rifle at the ready. We froze. Did he hear us, or was something else that woke him up? I looked to the front of the truck, and another German soldier was walking towards it. I heard them talk to each other, but I didn't understand what they were saying.

Sergeant Stevens said, 'Can you believe it's the mechanic?'

I just shook my head. We lay there for a few minutes. I looked up, and the hood was up, and both of them were leaning over the engine. Sergeant Stevens pointed to my right and motioned to start moving. The noise the soldiers were making allowed us to move faster.

Within just a few minutes, we were almost at the back of the truck. I looked both ways down the road and whispered, 'Looks clear.'

We both stood up and peered inside the truck. I pulled back the tarp, covering the truck bed's contents, revealing what it had been hiding. It was full of poison gas containers. I could tell by the skull and crossbones. We looked at each other, thinking the same thing. There was no way we were going to let that truck and its cargo proceed one inch."

I could see sweat forming on Patrick's face. His hand movements became more deliberate.

I asked Patrick, "Why would they leave a truck full of poison gas with only the driver, not a platoon or so to guard it?"

He took his hat off, scratched his head, and said, "I don't think they knew what was in the truck. Would you want to drive a truck loaded with poison gas? I wouldn't," he replied.

Put his hat back on and continued.

"The first thing we had to do was kill the German soldiers. I took out my trench knife and put my fingers through the knuckle guard. I saw Sergeant Stevens do the same. I duck-walked on the right, and he on the left. We both waited till we got to the front. In front of the truck were the two soldiers, smoking cigarettes and looking down the road. Neither of them was looking in our direction. I got up and ran toward the soldier with his right side to me. I put my hand around his neck and stabbed him, making quick thrusts in the back several times. I laid him on the ground.

At the same time, the German soldier Sergeant Stevens, who was going to attack, saw him out of the corner of his eye or heard something. The soldier turned toward him and knocked Sergeant Stevens to the ground. I lunged at the soldier with all my weight. He was a big guy. I grabbed him by his chin and pulled with all my might. I heard his neck snap. To make sure he was dead, I cut his throat. By now, Sergeant Stevens was back on his feet. He looked at me and said, 'Thank you, Patty.' I replied, 'We are both going to make it back.' We dragged them to the back of the truck and put them under the rear wheel axle."

Right then, Patrick got up with Sarge by his side and walked toward the front yard. After a couple of minutes, they both returned, and Patrick's head hung low.

Standing there, he said, "I didn't want to kill those soldiers, but I did what I had to do. Right?"

I replied, "Patrick, yes. You saved Sergeant Stevens' life. What would have happened if you didn't?"

"I wouldn't be here......"

After he said that, I thought to myself, *What did he mean by that? I wouldn't be here.*

He sat back down, and Pauline got up, going behind him to rub his shoulders. He looked up and said, "Thank you, dear. I love you."

She just smiled.

"Well, we each had two hand grenades left, and we each took one."

"Hold on, Patrick. You guys were going to blow up the truck with all those gas canisters in it?"

"We weren't going to, we did. We were hoping the fire and explosion caused by the grenades would incinerate the poison gas, causing it to be ineffective. We weren't sure, so we checked the wind direction, and luckily, it was blowing toward the Germans. Away from us or in the direction we were going to move. We put our gas masks on just in case, stepped away from the truck, pulled the pins, threw them in the back of the truck, and ran like hell. We only had five seconds before they would explode. So, we didn't run far before we hit the ground. While we were on the ground, we heard and felt them explode, one after another. I looked back after a couple of seconds, and the truck was engulfed in flames. We knew the Germans would see the explosion, and we wanted to move quickly away from the truck. So, with our gas masks on, we ran to the first building and waited.

When we arrived at the building, which I estimated was about a hundred feet away, we entered, sat down, looked at each other, shrugged, and removed our gas masks. I was out of breath and sweating profusely. When I took the damn thing off, my sweat poured out. We sat in silence, waiting for the poison gas to hit us. After a few minutes, we looked back at what was left of the truck again. The fire consumed it; all that was visible was the frame. There must have been more than those gas canisters it was carrying. After a few minutes, nothing. Sergeant Stevens took out his map and said, 'Okay, we are here, and we need to get here,' pointing to a location on his map. The way he was talking, it was like we just took a stroll in the park. My whole body was shaking."

"Well, did the gas become inert or did it kill some Germans?" I asked.

Patrick just sat there looking into space. Replied, "No idea. All I knew was we were both alive."

Pauline got up and asked, "How about some fresh iced tea?"

I replied, "Oh yes, that would be great. You, too, Patrick?"

He just sat there and nodded, not saying a word. At that time, I didn't know if he would continue. Recounting his story was taking a toll on him, not physically, but mentally.

Pauline pointed at me with her index finger and motioned for me to follow her into the house.

"Patty. Gordon is going to help me. Sit here and enjoy the weather. We will be right back."

Once in the house, she asked, "Should we let him continue?"

I replied, "With all due respect, Pauline. It's not up to us. I believe he wants to get it all out. He has been holding this inside for fifty years, fifty years."

Frowning, she replied, "Yes, you're right. Now come on, let's get the tea."

# CHAPTER 25

THE AMBUSH

Pauline and I walked out with the tea. Patrick was nowhere to be seen. Sarge was gone too, which made Pauline feel a little better. I put my glass down and walked off the porch. Next to the big tree were Sarge and Patrick.

I walked over and said, "Mind if I join ya?"

When I got beside him, he said, "Gordon, do you think this is too much for Pauline? I mean, she has never heard me talk like this."

I put my arm around his and said, "Well, Patrick, she is concerned that retelling your story is taking a toll on you."

He chuckled and said, "We are two peas in a pod. Come on, let's go back to the porch so I can tell the rest of my story."

Sarge led him back to the porch. I stayed back for a bit. I wanted him and Pauline to have a few minutes alone. As I stood next to the tree, I looked over to the porch. Pauline and Patrick were having a conversation. She leaned in, hugged him, kissed him, released him, and stroked his face with the back of her hand.

Pauline walked off the porch and said, "Gordon, come on. Patrick just told me the story is about to get good."

I cocked my head and thought, *about to get good?* I walked back to the porch, sat down, and picked up my tea. I took a drink and said, "Ready when you are."

As he started talking, I turned on my tape recorder.

"As we were in the building, thinking about our next move, out in front was some commotion. I got up and moved slowly to the door-frame, taking a quick look outside. To our front was a group of German soldiers, setting up a machine gun nest. They didn't look too concerned about being interrupted. There was no security at all. I went back and told Sergeant Stevens.

He said, 'Well, Patty, we need to get out of here. Let's check if there is a back door. I don't think it's a good idea to go out the front.' I couldn't have agreed more with his assertion.

So, we got our gear and moved to the back of the building. When we reached the back door, I positioned myself so that I could see down the alleyway. Sergeant Stevens slowly opened the door. As he did, the door made a creaking sound.

He stopped halfway opening it, looked at me, and whispered, 'Well, we've got to get out of here, and out the front door is not an option.'

He proceeded to open the door. Once it was open, we crouched down and listened for any movement. After a minute, we stood up and scanned left and right down the alleyway. It was all clear, so we started walking down it, being careful not to make any noise."

Patrick was starting to get a little nervous. I could hear it in his voice, but he kept talking.

"We had made it to where the alley dumped into a main street, and we crawled across it, making sure we stayed as low as possible so the gunner wouldn't see us. As we were about halfway, all hell broke out. Rat-tat-rat-tat-tat. Blue tracer rounds passed to our left and over our heads. We ran into an ambush.

Now I don't think it was put there for us, but it was there, and we were in the middle of it. I think we startled the machine gunners because their aim was way off. Either the gunner didn't see us, or he only heard something. Well, I still don't know to this day.

We both stayed on the ground, crawling even lower if that was even possible. After a few seconds, the machine gun fire stopped. But it was in a perfect position where we couldn't move back, left, right, or forward. We were stuck in a kill sack. I touched Sergeant Stevens on his shoulder and pointed to a wall about ten feet to our left. It would provide a little cover and concealment, allowing us to plan our next move, if we had one. I don't think 'planning' was the right word; we were acting on instinct—the most primal of survival modes.

As we made it to the wall, two of the German soldiers were right where we had just been. They were looking to see if they had wounded or killed anyone. They must have looked for two minutes before one of them said, 'Niemand hier. Du hast in die Luft geschossen. Du bist ein Schisser,' as they walked off.

Before I could ask what they said, Sergeant Stevens whispered, 'He said he was shooting at air, and they didn't find anyone. No one was there. The last part, I'm not for sure, never heard it before; must have been slang.

We both knew we couldn't just leave that machine gun nest there. When our soldiers moved down the street, they would be mowed down. They picked the perfect position.

Sergeant Stevens said, 'There are only two of them. I'm going to move around to their back and take them out. I need you to move forward, pick up a few bricks off the ground, and throw them down the street. They will start shooting. When they open up, I will take out the gunner and the assistant gunner, then meet over there—got it?' as he pointed to a building to our left.

I looked at him as if he were crazy. 'Excuse me, Sergeant, but do you think that's a good plan?' I asked.

His answer came very quickly: 'Do you have another. They are between us and the river.' He looked down at his watch. We only have two hours left.'

He handed me his leather pouch, which contained the map and the Top-Secret message. I put it around my neck and arm. He then pulled out a letter. The same one I saw him with before we even started this mission. He handed it to me and said, 'I want this back.'

I promised him that I would, once we linked up after he took out the machine gun next. I put it in my jacket pocket."

"Patrick, why didn't you put it in the pouch?" I asked.

"I knew when we handed over the pouch, they would take the pouch, and everything in it. It would be the last we saw of it. They would never let us take anything from it. Well, I knew if I put it in my jacket pocket, I could give it back to him. So, I put it in my pocket." He answered.

Even in the heat of the battle, Patrick was a very clear thinker.

"We both took deep breaths. He said, 'Give me two minutes' head start, then start moving and throwing the bricks.' I nodded, and we shook hands. I looked at my watch and began counting down the seconds. After two minutes, I started to move, after about forty feet. I picked up a brick and threw it into the street. Nothing, I picked up another and did the same. Still nothing, so I did what anyone else would do. I stood up and yelled, 'American Soldiers!' Got down and threw another. By the time the second one was out of my hand, bullets started flying down the street. Just as fast as the sound of bullets began, they stopped. I heard a couple of shots from the direction where the machine gun nest was. I looked up, and I saw Sergeant Stevens running toward me.

I looked at my watch to see how much time we had before the infantry squad was going to pick us up. With what little light there was, I could see it was 2236, only eighty-four minutes to get to the pick-up location. Time was not on our side.

All of a sudden, artillery shells started exploding all around me. They were relentless, but they didn't stop, boom, after boom. Even as the shells were raining in, Sergeant Stevens continued running toward me. Somehow, he made it to me. I asked him if he was okay.

He replied, 'Yep, I'm good.' But I saw otherwise. He was hit and bleeding. There was no time to treat him. We had to move. The shells were getting closer, so we took off. I was in front, and he was behind me. I just wanted to get us to the riverbank. From there, we had only a few more miles to go, but those three miles were going to be tough. The Germans knew we were here.

To this day, I still don't know if they knew we had the plans. If they did, they wanted those plans back, and they were out for blood. Our blood. I looked back, and he was right behind me. His shirt was covered in blood.

Suddenly, there was a shell that landed very close, and I was thrown through the air. My senses were overloaded. I lay there for what seemed like eternity."

# CHAPTER 26

I CAN'T SEE! I'M BLIND!

Pauline and I sat there as if we were in a trance—the vivid recall of Patrick was astonishing. As he told the horrific story, I was in awe at his bravery, self-control, and sheer grit.

I looked over at Pauline. Her breathing increased with every word Patrick uttered. She was there with him, all those many years ago.

Without skipping a beat or allowing me a chance to butt in, he continued, "As I lay there. I started to come around. I didn't feel any pain. Other than a slight headache. I felt my body for any warm, wet spots. Blood. Nothing, but everything was pitch black. I used a free hand to make sure my eyes were open, and they were. I started to panic, my heart began to race, beat after beat after beat. I felt like I was going to pass out. I was hyperventilating. I slowed my breathing and heart rate, trying to calm myself. I thought I must be covered in debris, and it was dark outside anyway. I pushed my left hand through the debris, and I could feel the wind on it. I moved what was on top of me and popped my head out. The cool breeze hit my face, and it felt so good, but I still couldn't see anything. I propped myself up, got my canteen, and poured some water on my eyes, but still nothing. I was blind. I yelled 'Sergeant Stevens,' over and over.

Finally, after a few seconds, I heard him.' 'Patty, are you okay?' I'm moving toward you.'

I replied, 'I'm blind. I can't see anything. I'm blind.'

It didn't take him a minute to reach me. He grabbed me by my shoulders and pulled me out from the rubble, and said, 'It's going to be temporary.'

'Yes, temporary,' I replied.

'Let me put this patch around your eyes. Hold still. I'll get ya to a doctor.' I could feel him starting to put the bandage around my head."

Patrick took off his sunglasses and rubbed his eyes.

I asked him, "Patrick, did you think your condition was temporary?"

"You know what? I didn't know if it was temporary. But I prayed that it was. We had guys in the unit who went blind from gas attacks, but never from artillery that I know of. For some of them, it was temporary, but many others weren't."

He put his sunglasses back on and continued.

"I was shaking. I thought I was going into shock as he finished putting a bandage around my head. I said, 'Thank you. Are you okay? I saw blood on your shirt.'

He replied in a very raspy voice, 'Not mine—one of the Germans.

I put my hand out. He grabbed and squeezed it. Then, he released it. I put my hand out again, but he didn't grab it. All I heard was, 'Get up, Patty, get out of here. I'll guide you.'

My legs were shaking. I got up and tripped over a brick or something, but I caught myself. In the distance to my rear, I heard the sounds of a German patrol moving in our direction.

'Patty, follow my voice. I will guide you.'

A calm came over me. To this day, I don't understand why or how. I was in the middle of the German territory and being hunted like an animal. Maybe I was resigned to being killed?"

Just then, Pauline got up and went inside the house.

"Who was that? Pauline, Pauline," cried Patrick.

Pauline came back outside, tears rolling down her face. "Patty, why didn't you ever tell me this? Why?"

"Honey, I knew how much it would disturb you. I never wanted to tell anyone. It was going to take it to the grave with me. I think I'll stop. Not much more to tell."

"Yes, it disturbs me, but that doesn't mean I wouldn't have tried to help or find you help. You helped so many veterans. Why wouldn't you let one of them help you? I want you to continue. You have to. You will never be at peace. I'm tougher than you think."

I dared not intervene. It was up to these two remarkable people to decide the next step.

Pauline and Patrick got up. Patrick took Sarge by his leash, and they walked off the porch and down the street, hand in hand. I sat there on the porch, closed my eyes, and took in the sounds of summer. Bees buzzing, birds chirping, and the rustling of leaves on the trees. I thought about my son and that he might have to fight in Vietnam. He only had two years left in college. I just hoped the damn war would end by the time he graduated. Because I knew since he was in Army ROTC, he would go. He would be the third generation of warriors, leading young men into battle.

I opened my eyes, grabbed my glass of iced tea, and watched as Pauline and Patrick walked back to their house. Without saying a word, they climbed the steps to the porch and sat down.

Hand in hand, he sat down, still holding her hand, and she sat down beside him. Sitting back in his chair, he continued, "I wanted to run to get as much distance between the Germans and us. But I knew if I did, I would only hurt myself and put Sergeant Stevens in more danger. I knew he was hit. I didn't know how bad it was or how fast he could move. I knew without my sight, I couldn't move fast. Since I only got a glance at him before I was knocked out, maybe it wasn't his blood on his shirt but that of one of the German soldiers, as he said.

I heard, 'Patty, I'm going to give you directions by using a clock. To your front is twelve, nine is to your left, six is behind you, and three is to your right. Now there is a ditch to your twelve o'clock, it's pretty deep, so go in slowly.'

Oh, how I wanted to move faster, but it was like something held me back.

'Patty, right in front of you, slowly.'

I almost got on my hands and knees to feel my way into the ditch. He was right, it was pretty deep, I would say five feet or so. Luckily, it was not very steep.

'Follow the ditch to your right.'

I put my hand out to feel the sides of the ditch. One to steady myself, the other for navigation. I thought, *How much further in this ditch?* It smelled horrific. I was ready at any time to trip over a dead body.

'Only a few more, Patty.'

I said, 'Sergeant Stevens. I have to stop, my head is killing me. I can't go on.'

'Patty, Okay. You can rest for a minute, but we have to keep going. The Germans are not going to stop looking for you.'

'I yelled, 'All right!'

I began to think that the temporary darkness wouldn't be temporary. At that time, I thought of you, Pauline. How or why would you still want me when I get back? To me, I was a broken man. I wouldn't be able to provide for you. At that moment, when I was feeling the most depressed I had ever felt, I felt a gentle breeze flow through me. A calmness. Not around me, but through me. The feeling of depression and pity, yes, pity, was gone. Since that time, I have never felt pity for myself again.

I got up and put my hand back on the side of the ditch and said, 'I want to go home, Sergeant Stevens.'

'You're about to exit the ditch. Once you are out, I'm going to take you into the woodline, then to the riverbank. Follow my voice.'

Every so often, he would make a sound, and I followed that sound out of the ditch to the woodline. That was the only way we communicated for some time. I never heard him complain or anything. I knew he had to be in pain, but there was nothing I could do. I didn't even have a rifle if the Germans found us. I had my M1911 pistol, four magazines, and one hand grenade.

'Patty, stop and get down. There are three Germans at our three o'clock at a distance of fifteen feet.'

I must have made a sound, because I could hear them moving toward me. I fumbled around for the grenade, pulled it off my belt, pulled the pin, threw it, and said, 'Get down.' I knew it would give away our position, but I was not going to let them capture us or kill us. It was my responsibility to get Sergeant Stevens and me back home.

The grenade exploded, and I must have either killed or wounded them because there was no movement from them anymore.

'Get up, Patty, and move.'

I followed his voice and sounds. As we went into the woodline, I smacked myself with a branch right in my eyes. I grabbed my face and dropped to one knee. The pain was like nothing I had ever experienced. I almost passed out again. But yet again, that cool breeze flowed through me. I got up and put my hands out in front of me, hoping to shield my face. I don't think I could have endured pain like that again.

We were moving at a good pace until I tripped over a fallen tree trunk. As I fell, I put out my hands to soften the blow. When my right hand hit the ground, it was pierced by a broken branch from a tree. It went right through my hand. I wanted to scream, but I didn't. I couldn't. I grabbed one end of the limb and pulled it out. The pain gripped my entire body. I quickly took my first-aid bandage from my equipment belt and wrapped it around the wound. I must have twisted my knee, because when I got up, I started to limp. I paused for a second."

Patrick held up his hand to show me the scar. I said, "I noticed it yesterday, but I didn't want to say anything."

Pauline looked at him and said, "Now I know the real story behind that scar."

Almost in an apologetic voice, he replied, "Well, I did say I got it in the war." Still holding hands, he squeezed it a little tighter.

He released her hand and continued.

"After I got up, I heard Sergeant Stevens say, 'Come on, Patty, almost out of the trees.' With my hands in front of my face, I continued to move until there were no more trees I could feel in front of me. I had a good feeling. Heck, if it weren't for being blind, a hell of a headache, a hole in my hand, and a sprained knee, I would have felt great."

I knew then I was not a reporter meeting a deadline. I was an observer of an ordinary soldier who did an extraordinary feat. The pain he endured would have broken any other man. But he was on a mission, and he was not about to fail. Not because he wanted to look good to the officers, get a medal, or any recognition, but for the soldiers. His friends who were killed in the last twenty-four hours. Rusty, Willy, Lar, and Scotty. With Sergeant Stevens wounded, he was singularly focused on getting himself and Sergeant Stevens back and giving the locations of his fallen friends so their bodies could be recovered and returned to their families, even if it killed him. I was in the presence of a real hero.

Pauline turned her attention to Patrick, got up, and without making a sound, walked over and clasped his face in her hands. She wiped away the sweat from his brow. Then gently kissed him on his forehead. She put her mouth to his ear and whispered something to him.

The smile on his face could have lit up a room.

# CHAPTER 27

TIME IS RUNNING OUT

We all just sat there for a few minutes, not saying anything. I looked down at my recorder, and the tape was almost at its end. I dug through my briefcase and found another blank tape. I pulled the tape out and wrote on it, "Patrick and Pauline King tape 3." As I shut the tape door, it clicked.

Patrick asked, "Did we already use up another whole tape?"

I replied, "Yep, you sure did."

He sat up, took a long, deep breath, let it out, and said, "When I looked at my watch before the explosion, we had less than two hours to arrive at the pickup location. It felt like we were in the forest for hours. I just knew we would miss the rendezvous time.

'Sergeant Stevens, what time is it?'

No reply, the silence was deafening. He didn't reply. I started to get very worried. Did we get separated? Was he lying somewhere, calling out my name?

I put my head down and said, 'I failed.'

Just as on the other couple of occasions, a cooling breeze ran through my body.

'Patty, almost out of the woods. Come on, follow my voice. Ten more feet, and then there is a clearing. Once through, the riverbank is right there. Follow it for a mile or so.'

His voice was soothing. There was no stress. He sounded at peace.

As I was walking, I had my arms out. I could feel trees and bushes to my left, right, and in front of me. Suddenly, I felt nothing. I stopped to confirm, and I conducted a 360-degree sweep. There are only trees behind me. I let out a sigh of relief. However, the ground was very uneven due to years of war; the terrain was pockmarked, and walking was more difficult than it was in the forest.

'Patty, come on. You have to move faster.'

I picked up the pace, stepped in a shell crater, and fell flat on my face. Luckily, there was at least half a foot of mud, so the fall wasn't too bad.

As I got up, I put my hand along the edge of the crater and felt cloth. At first, I couldn't figure out what I was touching. I moved my hand along the fabric. I felt cold flesh. I pulled my hand back and started to throw up. When I was done throwing up, I put my hands back on his body and moved them to the top of his head. He was wearing a Stahlhelm helmet—a dead German soldier. As I removed my hand from his helmet, a rat ran across my hand. I jerked it back and thought, *All I need is to get bitten by a rat and get an infection.*

I regained my composure, knelt, then got to my feet and stepped out of the shell crater. I was hoping I wouldn't fall into another one. I picked up my pace, then fell again. I got up, grabbed a wooden stick, moved my hands around it, and discovered it was a cross. I had stumbled into a graveyard. I got back on my feet slowly and made my way. I didn't want to fall again, but odds were I would.

'Patty, move to your eleven o'clock toward the bank.'

In the distance, to my left down the riverbank, I could hear movement. There was no time to run. I felt around for some tall grass and decided to hide in it. I leaped into the grass and lay down. I took my pistol out of its holster. I was not going without a fight. I couldn't hear Sergeant Stevens, so I assumed he did the same in front of me. As I lay there, the German patrol came closer and closer. They were saying something, but I couldn't make it out."

Sweat was pouring off Patrick's head. Pauline got up and wiped it away. "Honey, can you please get me a glass of cold water?" He asked.

"Of course, dear. Gordon, would you like one too?"

I replied, "Yes, but let me help you."

I walked into the house right behind her. She turned around and hugged me and said, "I never knew, I never knew. I could have done something, anything at all. I never knew."

I looked at her and replied, "What are you saying? You have no idea how you have helped him. You have been steadfast by his side. Remember when you told me he walked right by you at the train station? You could easily have missed the train and gone on without him. But you didn't, from that very second, stand next to him and help him live his life. A very productive one, I might add. There are many reasons veterans keep their war stories to themselves. Some don't want to appear weak to family, friends, or even fellow veterans. Or to spare them the utter brutality of war and what man can do to another man. For me, it was because I didn't want anyone to know I was the reason a young woman in France never grew old. I think he wanted to shield you from the reality of his war. He didn't want to upset you. Now come on, let's get a couple of glasses of cold water."

She didn't say anything. She cupped my face with her hands and smiled. We went into the kitchen, filled a couple of glasses with water, and added some ice. Carried them outside and sat one next to Patrick.

"Honey, are you okay?"

"Yes, Patty. I'm good."

He took a long drink from this glass, put it down, and continued his story.

"The German soldiers got closer and closer. It sounded like they went into the shell crater I was just in. Maybe they were there to recover their soldier. A couple of minutes later, it sounded like they stopped right in front of me. I slowed my breath, not moving a muscle. Suddenly, it felt like I was poked in the temple with a needle.

The pain was excruciating. I thought I was going to yell out. With my pistol in my hand, I brought it to my mouth."

"Stop, Patty. Stop!" Pauline cried out.

"What, Pauline? I wasn't going to kill myself. I bit down on the grip with all my might. Dear, I would have shot both of them. Sergeant Stevens and I had gone way too far to end it there. Like that, I'm going to continue, okay?"

"I'm sorry, Patty, and yes, please continue."

"They stood there and talked for what felt like a long time. The pain in my temple subsided. I released my grip on the pistol and waited for them to leave. I was praying they wouldn't move in the direction we had to move. We were running out of time to link up. I suppose God heard my prayer, and they began walking back in the direction they had come from. I waited until I couldn't hear them, and then I waited a couple of minutes more to ensure it was safe to move.

'Patty, it's safe—time to move.'

As I high-crawled in the field, the closer we got to the river, I could hear the rushing of the water. That is a sound I will never forget. I could feel the water's freshness and thought about how nice it would be to take a dip. Then I remembered the last time I saw the river, it was black water, filled with who knows what. I got up and walked crouching over."

I stopped him and asked, "Patrick, did it ever enter your mind that you might get shot at from the other side of the river?"

"Nope, for some reason, nope, not once. Well, a little later I did, and I had reason to."

He continued, "Now I knew we were running out of time, but we weren't stopping for anything. If we missed the boat, we still had the alternative escape route over the footbridge. 'Patty, you're about ten feet from walking into the river. Move at two o'clock.'

I turned to my two o'clock and kept low. Behind us, I could hear the sound of machine guns. Not German but ours. They must have opened up on the Germans who almost walked up on me. I froze in my tracks. My heart sank. The machine gunners didn't know we were on this side of the river. If they see us, they will fire on us. My whole body started shaking uncontrollably. Then I remembered the flare, and I felt around my utility belt, but it was no longer there. I must have dropped it earlier. I thought, *get all this way and get killed by our troops.*"

"Patty and Gordon, does that happen? Do American soldiers fire on other American soldiers?"

Patrick replied, "Sadly, yes, it does. There is so much chaos on the battlefield. We try to avoid it at all costs, but it does happen. It's called Friendly Fire."

Once Patrick was done answering Pauline's question. I said, "That is why it was so important that we knew where our soldiers were when we dropped ordinance. At times, they would pop smoke to let us know. But even with all the precautions, it happened."

"Thank you. I would have never thought of such a thing," replied Pauline.

Patrick took another drink from his glass, leaned forward, and said, "The machine gun fire stopped. We continued moving toward the link-up location. I had no idea how far we were from it. I was relying on Sergeant Stevens. As we moved, I heard a flare go off above us. I dove to the ground, not moving—rat, rat, tat, rat, the sound of machine gun fire at the top of the bank. I would hear the bullets impact.

I yelled, 'Sergeant Stevens, stay down.' Again, no reply. I assumed with all the noise, he didn't hear me. They must have fired hundreds of rounds in our direction even after they stopped shelling. I didn't want to move.

Then I heard Sergeant Stevens say, 'Patty, get up and move. It's right around the bend to your one o'clock. Twenty yards, almost there now, move, move. Take the flare gun out of the pouch.'

I reached into the pouch and felt the flare gun. I took it out. I had no idea how it got there. I pointed in the air and fired.

Without hesitation, I got up and ran as fast as I could in the direction he told me. I only tripped a couple of times. But we made it.

I could hear the voices of American soldiers. 'Lieutenant, I see'em to our right.'

I almost started to cry. I was so happy to hear another American's voice. 'Stop, Patty, you're here.' I stopped.

"I felt myself falling."

Patrick got up from his chair with Sarge next to him. He walked down to the end of the porch. He stood there, leaning his head back without moving. He put his head down and returned to his seat. He put his hand in his pocket and pulled out a snack for Sarge. He reached his hand out, and Sarge took the treat ever so gently.

Then he said, "I'm getting hungry. What time is it?"

I looked down at my watch and answered, "Wow, it's almost noon. Time is flying."

"Gordon, would you mind if we had sandwiches again?" Pauline asked.

"Are you kidding. I loved them yesterday. Can I help ya?"

"No, no, thank you. I'll be right back. Patrick, do you need anything?"

He rubbed his chin and replied, "Well, after lunch, I sure could use a piece of that apple pie and some ice cream."

I thought to myself, 'That sounds good.'

Pauline walked over to him, kissed him on his forehead, and said, "Only if you eat all of your sandwich."

She didn't wait for an answer. Pauline already knew it, and she walked into the house, smiling.

# CHAPTER 28

BACK ACROSS THE MARNE

As Patrick and I sat outside, we remained silent. Every now and then, a car would pass in front of the house, and the driver would honk. It seemed everyone in Bald Knob knew Patrick and Pauline. But Pauline and I were the only ones who knew his story. One he had kept buried for fifty years. Patrick took off his hat and wiped his forehead with a handkerchief from the front pocket of his shirt.

"Getting warm today. Going to be a scorcher," Patrick said as he put his hat back on and put the handkerchief back in his pocket.

I replied, "Yep. The humidity is one thing I don't think I will ever get used to. I thought North Texas was bad."

"Gordon, I have lived here my entire life, and I'm not even used to it."

Pauline walked out of the house with a tray full of sandwiches, chips, and three RC Colas. As she put the tray on the small table, she said, "So, what were ya'll talking about?"

Patrick answered, "The weather. Gordon said he can't get used to the humidity."

Laughing, she replied, "Me neither. Now dig in."

She picked up one of the sandwiches and put it, along with some chips, on a paper plate. "Patrick, put out your hand, and I will hand you your lunch. I'll put the RC Cola on the table next to you."

I picked up the RC Cola and took a swig. I swallowed and said, "Wow, that is good."

"What? Gordon, you have never had an RC Cola before?" Asked Pauline.

I shook my head and said, "Nope. But I will now."

We sat and ate lunch in silence.

"Pauline, look, I ate everything! It's time for pie and ice cream," said Patrick.

"Well, can it wait till we are done?" Asked Pauline.

"Of course, honey. I'm not going anywhere."

Once we were all done, Pauline went inside and got each of us a piece of her apple pie and a scoop of ice cream. We sat there and enjoyed every morsel.

"Pauline, can I get another one of those RC Colas?" I asked. "Of course, Gordon. They are in the refrigerator.

I went inside, opened the refrigerator, and took one. I went back outside and waited for Patrick to start up again.

Patrick finished his ice cream and put the plate on the table. He took a drink from his cola and said, "I must have fallen and hit my head when I tried to get into the boat. I woke up in the boat. I'm not sure how I got in, but as I lay there in the boat, the sound of artillery shells hitting the bank of the river filled my head. I didn't know whether I was dreaming or awake. I felt water on me. It was the spray from shells hitting the water.

I tried to get up, but one of the soldiers pushed me back down and said, 'Keep your head down.'

Machine gun fire echoed off both sides of the boat. The Germans targeted the boat. "Row faster, zig zag, faster,' yelled one of the soldiers. One of the soldiers was firing his BAR at the Germans.

Another responded, 'Sir, we are rowing as fast as we can. The current is pushing us away from our exit point.'

I started yelling, 'Sergeant Stevens. Sergeant!'

Another soldier who was not rowing the boat began shooting. The shells were all around us. The boat started to take on water. A bullet or shrapnel must have hit us. I could feel it on my back.

I sat up again and said, 'The pouch, it's around my neck. Ensure the pouch reaches headquarters. Screaming at the top of my lungs, I said, 'Do you hear me? ' to headquarters! Did Sergeant Stevens get in the boat? Did he?'

No one answered. I'm not even sure I was saying it out loud. I was in a daze. I didn't know where we were on the river. It seemed we had been underway for a long time. I remembered back just a few hours ago when the patrol rowed across it. It only took us a few minutes.

'Come on, men, we are almost there. Row, row,' all this time the artillery was still shelling us. Machine guns were firing all around us. I felt the boat hit its bottom on the bank.

'Get up, soldier,' I heard someone say, and then I felt someone grab me and hurry me out of the boat. 'Come on faster, faster.' I replied, 'I'm blind. I'm moving as fast as I can!'

'Private, I'm going to take the pouch from around your neck," one of the soldiers said.

'Private Mitchell, take this pouch and get it to headquarters at all costs. Now go. Private McCormick, you go with him. One of you better make it.'

Two of the other soldiers put their arms under mine and hauled me up the bank. As we were, I guess, halfway, one of the soldiers released his grip and fell to the ground. He had been hit. Another soldier took his place, and we raced up the bank. As we ran, I could hear the tearing of cloth. We were moving through the barbed wire, a gap the engineers had opened for us. I knew I would be back in the trenches before long. My heart was pounding faster and faster. I thought it was going to pop out of my chest."

Suddenly, Patrick grabbed his chest.

"Patty, are you okay. I'll get your medicine." Pauline ran into the house.

I jumped up and went over to Patrick, put the cool RC Cola bottle on the back of his neck, and asked, "Patrick, are you having a heart attack?"

He smiled and said, "Yes, but it's a little one."

"A little one?"

"Yes, I had a major heart attack a couple of years ago."

Pauline was back on the porch in a flash. "Give me your open hand." He put his open hand out. She put a pill in it and said, "Take it now."

He popped the pill in his mouth and sat back.

"Why didn't you guys tell me Patrick had a heart condition. I wouldn't have pressured him into giving the interview."

"Pressure me? Gordon."

"He does have a heart condition, but the nitroglycerin will help him. If not, we can take him to the hospital in Searcy. Patrick, are you feeling better?

Gordon, would you drive us if we need to go?" Asked Pauline.

It didn't take me a second to reply, "Yes, yes, of course." I put my hand in my pocket and pulled out my car keys.

"Patrick, how do you feel?" Asked Pauline again. I was already moving to my car.

"Yes, dear, I'm much better. We can start back in a few minutes." I stopped in my tracks when I heard him say that.

"You want to finish, Patrick?"

"Oh hell yes. I've gone too far to stop now."

A few minutes passed, and both Pauline and I watched Patrick, making sure he was feeling okay.

"Alright, here we go. We stopped, and one of the soldiers told me to get on his back. I asked, 'You are going to carry me?'

'Yes, it will be safer and a hell of a lot quicker,' he replied.

He turned around and went down one of the ladders into the trench. I could instantly smell the stench of the trench. But for some reason, I finally felt safe. He put me down and said, 'Stretcher Bearer over here.'

I pulled at his arm and said, 'Where is Sergeant Stevens?' The other soldier who was with me!' Where is he?'

I heard, 'I don't know who you are talking about.'

Before I could answer, I felt dizzy and slumped forward. I felt like I was being put on the stretcher and being hauled off. In my head, I kept asking, *Where is Sergeant Stevens? Where is he?*"

# CHAPTER 29

TRIAGE

As the day wore on, I could see that Patrick was growing increasingly tired. I knew he wanted to go on, but I was concerned about his health. However, there was no way we were going to stop him from completing his story. Pauline got up and filled his glass of water, leaned into him, and whispered something. I didn't hear what, but he nodded his head.

Pauline had gone into the house, brought out a folding chair, and placed it at Patrick's feet.

"Honey, put your feet up for a bit," she commanded.

He put his feet on the chair and started up again, "I woke up as one of the medical team at the Battlefield Aid Station started taking off my bandage covering my eyes.

'Private, can you hear me?"

I nodded and said, 'Yes, but I can't see you. I can't see anything.'

'Yes, I can see there is some damage to your eyes. Do you know what happened?'

'All I recall is the artillery shells impacting. I was thrown some distance, woke up, and couldn't see.'

'I'm going to have you moved to the Advanced Dressing Station. There, they will clean your eyes and replace the bandage I'm going to put on. Okay? You're going to be fine.'

I started to bring my hands to my eyes, but he pulled them back and said, 'Try not to rub your eyes. Strecher Beares, take him to the ADS. No, never mind, take him directly to the Casualty Clearing Station (CCS).'

The stretcher bearers picked me up and loaded me into an ambulance. I must have dozed off, or maybe they gave me something to sleep, I don't know."

* * *

"I dozed in and out of consciousness. However, the longer we drove, the more awake I became, and I realized the roads were terrible. Ruts and Potholes everywhere. I could feel each one in my head as they drove over them. However, I must say that those soldiers were exceptional. The care they took with not only me but with every soldier was exceptional. The ambulances had big red crosses on the sides and top. They were an excellent target for the German planes. I'm so glad I didn't hear any planes.

I don't know how far we drove, but I do know it was some distance from the front lines. When we stopped, I asked, 'Is Sergeant Stevens in another ambulance?'

One of them replied, 'We don't know. I can ask when we arrive.'

At least this time, someone acknowledged his existence."

When Patrick was talking about the Stretcher Bearers, he seemed more relaxed than when he was in combat. He was more comfortable and not as anxious.

"They took me out of the ambulance and took me into the Casualty Clearing Station. They picked me up and took me off the stretcher and onto an examination table.

'Soldier, I'm Doctor Gray. I'm going to take your bandage off.'
I didn't say anything.
As he was taking it off, he asked, 'Do you hurt anywhere else?'

I replied, 'No,' at first, then I held my hand up.'

'Okay, I'm first going to look at your eyes, then your hand.'

Once the bandage was off, he asked, 'Can you see the light?'

I shook my head, no.

I could feel the doctor pull my eyelids wide—first the right, then the left.

He said, 'There is nothing in your eyes, a little dust, but that wouldn't prevent you from seeing. I don't see any trauma. Let me know if where I'm touching hurts.'

He started at my right temple and moved around my head. When he got around to touching the back of my head. I let out a scream. 'Okay, soldier. I'm done touching, but I need to lift your head.'

I braced myself for the pain I knew I was in for when he raised my head. But there was none; he was very gentle.

'Hmm. Saline solution and a cotton wipe.'

As soon as he poured the solution and dabbed with the cotton wipe, it almost lifted me off the table. But I didn't say anything; hell, maybe I was in shock.

'Classify Private King as terrible,' shouted the doctor.

I could feel him bend over me.

He said, 'Soldier, you have at least one piece of shrapnel in your skull. I think it's putting pressure on your occipital lobe. It's responsible for controlling sight. That is why you are blind. Now, I don't know if it's temporary or permanent. I don't know, and I don't have the right equipment to take it out and verify. You need to go to the hospital in Paris. You're going to be evacuated within the next hour.'

I just lay there, not saying a word.

'I'm going to put some drops in your eyes, then put the bandage back on.'

He then took my wounded hand, pulled off the bandage, 'Hmm, it's infected. I'm going to wash it out, clean it with sodium hypochlorite, and provide you with a treatment to address the infection. It should take care of it. It will need some stitches. Now this is going to sting.'

Suddenly, I heard, 'Ten-hut. At ease, men.'

I heard footsteps coming toward me. I then felt a hand on my shoulder.

'Private King, I'm Major General Nolan. I was the one who briefed you last night. You and the rest of your men did an outstanding job. The intelligence you provided is worth its weight in gold. I can't go into it, but many lives will be saved.'

I didn't want to talk to him, but I needed some information.

'Where is Sergeant Stevens. He was with me on the boat. Where is he? Is he okay? I have something to give him.'

'Private, you were alone. I debriefed the squad that picked you up. You were the only one at the link-up point. They say they waited for a few minutes, but when the artillery began firing, they had to depart and cross the river again. They didn't see anyone but you.'

I sat up and said, 'No, he was with me. He guided me to the link-up point. I want to speak with him, please. He saved my life. There is no way I could have made it to the pickup point after the artillery attack that blinded me. We were miles away in a village. Please explain to me how I made it from the village, through the forest, across the field, down the riverbank, and then along it to a certain point. Blind. I can't see anything, now explain that! I have to talk to him. I have a letter that I promised to return to him. It's in my pocket.'

'General, do you have any information on Sergeant Stevens?' The doctor asked.

He never gave a response. If he did, it was with his head.

'By the way, General, whoever was going to meet us never showed up. We waited a few minutes, but he never showed up. Hear me? Never showed up. Sergeant Stevens continued the mission without him. He never showed up.'

I felt a hand squeezing my shoulder, 'Thank you, Private, for letting me know. We thought he was the one who guided you. We knew there would be no way a patrol could make it without his help.'

'We weren't just a patrol, General. We were Sergeant Stevens' patrol.'

I heard ten-hut and footsteps."

Patrick, "You never found out who it was that was supposed to meet your patrol, did you?" I asked.

He replied, "No, never did."

"I sat up, as my head felt like it had been split in half. At that time, I thought, Why, why now is it hurting? I mean, I tripped and fell, stumbled all the way to the pickup point, but never felt that level of pain on a scale of one to ten; it was twenty. Just as quickly as I had been in pain, it was gone. I felt that breeze. The same breeze flowed through my body again. The pain was gone.

'Soldier, sit back and try to relax,' said the doctor.

I felt a hand go into my pocket.

I shouted, 'No, leave it. Don't touch it. I'm going to give it to him. I promised him. Where is he?' The rage inside of me was building."

The calmness we saw earlier was gone. He was visibly upset.

"Calm down, Patrick, please?" Asked Pauline.

"I haven't thought of being in the field hospital in years. I put it so far back in my memory. When it surfaced, I was just as mad. I'm okay now. Sorry."

"Sorry, Patrick, for what? There is nothing to be sorry about. I would have been upset, too. Do you know why they weren't giving you any information on Sergeant Stevens?" I asked.

He put his head down, took off his hat, and stretched out his legs on the chair. Sarge got up and, like before, put his head in his lap. Patrick started patting him with one hand, while with the other, he put his hat back, lifted his head, and said, "That comes later. At that time, I didn't know. They had a war to fight, and worrying about one soldier was not a priority to them, but to me, it was my highest priority. I had to find out. I had to." He wiped a tear from his eyes.

"However, they put their hand in my pocket and took it out.

I yelled, 'Put it back! It's my responsibility, not yours!'

"Whoever took it out put it back and said, 'Okay, okay,' and put the letter back.'

I heard, 'Can you give him something?'

I felt a warm fluid going through my veins.

'The last thing I heard was, 'Get ready for a large number of casualties'

As I drifted off, I thought, maybe he wasn't wounded, and he didn't need any assistance. He was already back with the platoon. He was alright. I just wanted the opportunity to thank him in person. I had to give his letter back to him. I promised. I would have never made it back and into the hospital without him, my hero."

# CHAPTER 30

LAID UP IN THE HOSPITAL

While in the Casualty Clearing Station, the pain and anguish of not knowing the whereabouts or condition of Sergeant Stevens were palpable now in Patrick's expressions and words. I didn't understand why they wouldn't tell him anything. Was it to shield him in his condition, or did they not know what happened to him? Was he missing in action? In the service, it's sometimes hard to tell. It might have been all about the information he brought back.

Patrick picked up his glass. Pauline noticed it was empty. "Hold on, Patrick, let me get you some fresh lemonade. Gordon, would you like some too?"

There was no way I was going to turn that down. "Yes, please."

"That would be wonderful, honey. Thank you," said Patrick.

While Pauline was in the house, Patrick asked me, "Gordon, when I was getting medically evaluated by the doctors and staff, I kept asking where Sergeant Stevens was. But they never gave me an answer, so I kept asking myself why they wouldn't tell me anything about Sergeant Stevens."

I replied, "I was asking myself the same question."

Pauline walked out of the house with two lemonades. The puzzled look on my face must have given it away.

She looked at me and pulled out an RC Cola from her dress pocket. Handed it to me, smiled, and said, "I know you love these."

"Yep, my new favorite drink. Well, that and beer."

"Beer?" Said Patrick.

I replied, "Yes, sorry if I offended you."

They both started laughing. "Gordon, if you want a beer, we have a few in the fridge."

"Well, I haven't opened the cola yet," I said.

Pauline got up, and she was about to walk into the house, when Patrick said, "I'll take one too. The doctor said I can have one."

"Yeah, I never heard him say that," she replied,

Patrick smirked and said, "He must have said it when you were out of his office."

She shrugged her shoulders and walked inside. Not more than two minutes later, she walked out with three cans of Schlitz. She handed them all to me and said, "Here is the can opener."

I took the opener, popped out two holes in the tops of the cans, one larger on one side and one smaller on the other. I did it one by one. After they were all open, I held up my can and said, "Friends don't let friends drink alone." We tapped our cans together, and I said, "To the most beautiful couple I have ever met. Cheers."

"Man, that's so good," said Patrick. He put the can down on the table and continued his story.

"I don't know how long I was in the Casualty Clearing Station, but when I woke up, I was in another ambulance. This time, the roads were so much better. I wasn't getting bounced around. As I woke up, I heard, 'You're awake, how do you feel?'

It was a voice I had never heard before. I replied, 'I guess the same. Who are you?'

'Sorry, I'm Private Thomas. I'm going to the American Hospital with you. There are two others with us. Both of them are out. One doesn't look good.'

'Can you do me a favor?' I asked.

'Sure, what?' He replied.

'What are their names. Can you tell me what they are?'

'I guess. The fella over you is, let me see, Sergeant Stratford. Give me a second, the other guy is Corporal Wallace. Are you looking for someone in particular?'

'Yes, but they aren't him. Thanks for looking. Do you know where we are headed?'

'Yep, Paris.'

* * *

"The one thing I noticed as we drove to Paris was the quietness—no machine guns, rifles, or artillery. At that time, I thought *I was going to make it out of here.* The sounds of Paris' hustle and bustle shattered the tranquility of the ride. The sound of car horns and people yelling - I was so happy to hear every car horn and the yelling. I hadn't been back to Paris since I got to France. We went straight to training, then off to the front. I wish I could have seen it again. But that was not going to happen.

We stopped, and they opened the back doors. I could feel the breeze, but best of all, I could smell the scent of Paris. I couldn't see it, but heck, I was going to enjoy the smell.

Private Thomas was the first one out. He could walk. You know, I never asked him about his wound. I guess because he never asked me. The soldier above him was next. As the orderlies were about to take the soldier above me, I heard one of them say, 'Leave him. Let's get the blind guy out. This one is dead.' I prayed for him."

Patrick leaned forward, picked up his beer, took another drink, and said, "You know, something, it seemed every time I got my spirits up, I would be pulled back into darkness. There was no escaping the war. Soldiers died everywhere."

He took off his hat and put the cold beer across his forehead. He took his feet off the chair and leaned back. He took another drink and put his hat back on.

"They started to carry me in, but I stopped and said, 'I can walk. Let me walk. Please guide me.'

'Okay, put your hand on my shoulder. We are going to walk inside and meet one of the doctors who will be taking care of you while you're here.'

I replied, 'Thank you.'

'Put him over here,' I heard someone say. I guessed it was the doctor.

'Hello, welcome to the American Hospital of Paris. I'm Doctor William Keen Jr., Major, U.S. Army. Forget about the Major, call me Doctor Keen or Doc Keen. I'll be looking after you while you're in Paris.'

'Hi, Doctor Keen. Am I going to be blind the rest of my life?' I asked him.

'Well, I'm not going to sugarcoat any of my prognoses. I'm going to be direct. Hell, what you went through at the front, you're lucky to be alive. I read your report. You're going to be okay. But right now, I don't know till I examine you.'

'Deal, Doc Keen.'

'I see in your records that you lost your sight during an artillery attack with no other injuries, correct? Oh, hold on, you also have a hand injury. It doesn't say where you were wounded.'

'Yes, sir, my head and my hand, it was near Château-Thierry along the Marne.'

'I didn't think there was much fighting going on now,' said Dr. Keen.

'Well, I was with a patrol that was on the German side of the river.'

'Okay, how far were you from friendly lines when you lost your sight?' Doctor Keen asked.

'Hmm, three miles or so. We got hit by artillery in a small village. I went through a forest, an open field, down the banks of the Marne, then along it to a pick-up point.'

'You said, we. What happened to the other soldiers?'

Rusty drowned in the Marne, Willy stepped on a mine, which blew him in half, and the Germans killed Lar and Scotty. Sergeant Stevens and I were the only ones left. He is the one who got me back to the pickup point.'

'So, you and Sergeant Stevens? What happened to him?'

'I have no idea. I asked about him back at the front. But they said he never made it to the boat.'

I heard Doctor Keen mumble, 'Then how did you make it all that way?'

'Let me make some calls to see if I can get some information on Sergeant Stevens. Do you know his full name?'

'Yes, James W. Stevens.'

'Now, let me look at you. Please lie down and turn over on your stomach.'

After checking me out, he told me, You have some shrapnel in your skull. I'm going to get some X-rays to see how many there are and whether I can remove them.

He did a more extensive exam, then called for one of the nurses to take me to get some X-rays of my head. It only took a couple of hours to complete them. Once I was done, they wheeled me to my room. By the sound of it, there must have been ten or more soldiers in it."

* * *

"I must have dozed off and slept for a couple of days. I only woke up when a nurse shook my shoulder.

'Private King, you have a visitor.'

I thought it was Sergeant Stevens.

I then heard Doctor Keen, 'Patrick, how do you feel?'

'The same, but rested. Now, how long did I sleep?' I asked.

'Almost three days. We checked on you, but didn't want to wake you. Rest is the best medicine. I'm here because someone would like to meet you. He is outside. How about we put you in a wheelchair and take you out?'

I knew it was Sergeant Stevens. There was no way he would see me in a wheelchair. I was walking out.

'Doctor Keen, I want to walk out. No wheelchair.'

'Nurse, please escort him out. Patrick, I'll meet you out there and go over my prognosis and treatment.'

I got dressed and then said, 'Where is my letter. I had a letter with me. I told them to leave it with me. Where is it?'

I heard a drawer open, 'Private King, here it is. I put it in the drawer.'

I reached out my hand, and she placed the letter in it. I put it in the pocket of the "Hospital Blues." I put both my arms out and asked, 'Can I give you a hug?'

She replied laughing, 'Well, if it's alright with Pauline. You were calling her name over and over the other night.'

After a very quick hug, she escorted me outside."

Pauline got up and almost ran over to Patrick. When she got there, she said, "Stand up, soldier." He stood up, and they must have hugged for five minutes. It was like they hadn't seen each other for years."

# CHAPTER 31



They released each other. Patrick sat back down and continued.

"Well, I walked out the doorway of the hospital. I could feel the sun on my face and a cool breeze. It felt so good. I heard Doctor Keen say, 'Over here, bring him over here.'

When we arrived, I heard a familiar voice I never wanted to hear again: Major General Nolan.

'Private King, I want to introduce you to General Pershing.' At first, I thought I was hearing things. Why would General Pershing visit me, a Private, a nobody? However, I did have one question for him, and if I had the opportunity to ask, I would."

'Private King, please sit down,' I assumed it was General Pershing.

The nurse grabbed me by my shoulders and maneuvered me to the bench. I sat down. I could hear someone else sitting next to me.

He started talking, 'I want to let you know that the mission your squad conducted the other night provided us with critical information and plans for a German attack. With the information, we were able to develop effective battle plans and deploy the right forces to put up an intense fight. That put the Germans on the run. The information you brought back saved countless allied lives. In addition, cutting the communication lines disrupted their ability to command and control their units at the front. So, with that, can you please stand?'

I stood up at attention.

Private King, you are now promoted to the rank of Corporal for exceptional service to the war effort, allied nations, and the United States. Effective date 1 July 1918. In addition, I'm awarding you the Distinguished Service Cross for gallantry above the call of duty.'

I could feel him pin it on my robe."

"Patrick, do you know that is the second-highest award that can be awarded to a service member? It's right under the Medal of Honor."

"Pauline, can you please go into my top drawer and get the small blue box way in the back, please?"

Pauline got up and went into the house. She walked back out with the little blue box in her hand. "Can I open it, Patrick?" She asked.

"Yes, of course."

She opened the box and pulled out the Distinguished Service Cross (DSC). At the top portion, the ribbon has a thin red vertical line, a thin white vertical line, and a middle blue ribbon featuring a bronze cross with an eagle attached. She held it up and said, "I never knew what this was or why you had it."

"I know, honey. I haven't pulled it out in fifty years. I never thought I deserved it."

"Why would you think that, Patrick? What you and your squad accomplished was unsung bravery. Everyone should have gotten one posthumously," I said.

He replied, "As far as I know, they all received Silver Stars."

"Why wasn't the awarding of your medal in the news in the local or state papers?" Asked Pauline.

"It was a secret mission. No one was to know. Heck, when he awarded it to me, the nurse had to step back out of hearing range."

"I'm proud of you, Patrick," said Pauline.

"Well, let me continue, 'I said, Sir, I don't deserve this. Sergeant Stevens is the one who got us there and me back. If it weren't for him, you would never have had those plans. Did you give him one too?'

'Patrick. Mind if I call you Patrick?' Asked General Pershing.

'No, sir, not at all.

'Here, let me help you sit.' He grabbed me by my arms and sat me back on the bench. Once I was settled, he sat next to me. I felt him move closer to me.

'Patrick, I know you have been asking about him, so I authorized a search and rescue mission, using the detailed information on the map in the pouch you brought back. Of course, the patrol started at the banks of the Marne and worked its way back to the OP. When they got to the village, his body was recovered.'

'Wait, no, no, no. Was his body recovered in the village? I felt him and touched him. He was alive.'

'I had him identified by one of the Mortraray teams. He was positively identified by his identification disks around his neck and by the Company Commander. Patrick, Sergeant Stevens, was killed in that village. Hours before you got to the pick-up point.'

'Then how did I make it back? I can't even walk across this area without stumbling, running into something, or falling.'

I got up and started walking. I made it five feet before I tripped and fell. "Private King, stop where you are,' said Doctor Keen.

'Did you see, did you? I can't walk without falling. How did I make it back? It makes no sense.'

By then, my head was spinning. Back then, I couldn't explain how I felt. But today, I would have a carousel going round and round, and I couldn't get off."

Patrick was clearly agitated. Pauline and I sat and looked at each other.

"Doctor Keen ran over to me and helped me up. As he did, he asked, 'What are you trying to prove?'

'He led me to the pickup point. To me, he was right there and alive. But now you're telling me he was dead. How is that even possible?' My mind went back to the village when I asked him if he had been hit, and he replied no. Then, he grabbed my hand. But that was the last time I touched him.

Doctor Keen took me back to the bench. I sat down. 'Patrick, are you a religious man?' Asked General Pershing.

'Yes, I think I am. I try to live right and believe in God.'

'I'm a lot older than you and have been in many battles and seen things I can't explain. With what I can't explain, I leave those to God and his wisdom. I think your arrival at the pickup point was one of those things that can't be explained. God was watching over you through Sergeant Stevens' soul, spirit, whatever you want to call it. Some would say divine providence.'

I replied, 'I wanted so for him to be alive. I would be dead if not for him.'

'Patrick, there are many stories like yours where fallen soldiers aided soldiers. However, I must say that yours is the most extraordinary I have ever heard. I don't doubt you for one second that everything you have said happened. I think it happened. Now, with that, I wouldn't go around saying anything. If you do, there will be some, hell, many that will label you insane. I recommend keeping this to yourself. Plus, your patrol was on a top-secret mission.'

'Additionally, I would like to inform you that former President Theodore Roosevelt expresses his gratitude for bringing back his son Quentin's identification disk and verifying his death.'

I replied, 'Sir, we saw him get shot down. There was no way Sergeant Stevens or I were going to leave him there. We had to verify he was dead. If he weren't, we would have brought him home, General. Leave no man behind.'

General Pershing got up and patted me on the back. Leaned down and said, 'Patrick, you were worth saving.'

Well, from that day till you came here yesterday, Gordon. I have never revealed the story of how Sergeant Stevens saved my life."

No one said a word. I was letting the last day and a half sink in. Patrick's ability to tell his story so vividly made me feel like I was part of it.

"Well, let me finish up. Doctor Keen and the nurse took me back into an observation room and sat me down.

As I sat on the exam table, Doctor Keen said, 'Patrick, I got the X-rays back, and I can try to go in and get the shrapnel, but I'm not sure if you would regain your sight or even make it through the operation.'

'So, I'm going to be blind the rest of my life.'

'Yes, I'm afraid so. I'm sorry, but there is really nothing I can do. With that, you will be transferred to a rehabilitation hospital in England. There you will be taught to take care of yourself, get around, and learn Braille. There is no reason you can't live a full life, with I hear her name is Pauline.'

Why would she want me back? I'm not the man I was. I can't take care of her. I'm an invalid.

'Alright, Private King. I have had enough. That stunt outside, and now you're feeling sorry for yourself. You listen to me. You are not an invalid. Do you know how many young men like yourself, who have no arms or legs, can't walk or talk? Hell, there are some whose wounds are buried in their heads. They relive their battle every day. Have you ever heard of 'Shell Shock'? Want to know something? There is a young soldier here who, when he sees a helmet, can't control his bowel movements. I'm sorry if I don't have much sympathy for you. There is a reason you are here and not dead like Sergeant Stevens, Lar, Willy, Scotty, and Rusty. Now, stop feeling sorry for yourself and have a productive life. You owe them; that is how you repay them. Nurse, please prepare him for transfer to England.'

When he was talking to me, I could hear the pain in his voice. Never in a million years, when he was in medical school, did he think he would be treating people with wounds never seen before. I knew he would be living with the war forever.

As the nurse walked me out of the observation room, I said, 'Doctor Keen, I'm sorry, and thank you.' I started feeling better about myself. I still wasn't sure about the relationship with Pauline. One thing I knew and was sure of was that I would not let Sergeant Stevens, Lar, Scotty, Willy, or Rusty down."

Patrick looked in Pauline's direction and said, "You are the best thing that has ever happened to me. I love you. I'm sorry for those many years ago when I doubted you."

"Patrick Wayne King, "I have loved you since the day you fell at my feet."

"Excuse me, I tripped."

We all started laughing.

"Well, I made it to the rehabilitation hospital, and just as Doctor Keen said, they taught me to read Braille, I was taught how to use a cane, and I'm pretty self-sufficient. Right, Pauline? Well, that's about it, Gordon. That's my story. No, not my story. It's Sergeant Stevens, Lar, Willy, Rusty, and Scotty's story."

I turned off my recorder, removed the tape, and put it in my pocket. I stood up and went over to Pauline. As I walked over, she stood up. I said, "Pauline, I can't thank you enough for all you've done to make me feel like part of your family."

She said, "You are like a son, Gordon."

Pauline got up and said, "Hold on for one second."

Pauline walked into the house, and within a minute, she was back on the porch with a photograph in hand. I looked at it. A picture of Patrick the day he left for France.

I lowered the picture and said, "Wow, Patrick was a very handsome young man."

Patrick asked, "Pauline, did you show him that picture?"

"Yes, I sure did. You were so handsome in your uniform. Gordon, you're welcome to use it in your article if you'd like. All I ask is that you bring it back."

I put the photograph in my shirt pocket.

I gave her a peck on the cheek and said, "Yes, I will put it in the article, and I will definitely bring it back."

I walked over to Patrick, and he started to get up, but I said, "Please stay seated."

"Hell no. I'm standing. Son, I can't thank you enough. I feel like a new man. I always wanted to tell this story, but I was afraid I would be judged. Somehow, with you, I knew you wouldn't. I trusted you."

"Patrick, you are the one to thank. Your story is one I will never forget, and even though I want to tell it in the paper, I won't. I don't want anyone to judge you. You will be part of it, but some things are between you, me, Pauline, and the porch."

He replied, "Don't forget, Sarge. Thank you, son."

"And Sarge!"

I gave him a hug, bent over, and stroked Sarge's head. I saw something in his eyes.

I grabbed all my stuff and walked off the porch.

As I got to my car, I heard, "Breakfast is at seven."

I stopped in my tracks. Turned around and asked, "Sarge is named after Sergeant Stevens, isn't he?"

"I was wondering when you were going to ask that question. Yes, every one of my dogs' names has been Sarge," Patrick replied.

I said, "Makes sense, and I will see you in a couple of weeks."

I got in my car and drove off. With my mouth watering, thinking about breakfast, I stopped at "Buds Grocery", which I had stopped at yesterday. I went in and bought two RC Colas. As I was paying, the same young man from yesterday said, "You might as well get a Moon Pie to go with your RC Colas."

I replied, "Moon Pie?" He reached over the counter and handed me one. I looked at it, then at him, smiled, and took it, paying him.

As I walked out the door, he asked, "What did you and the Kings talk about?"

I answered, "You wouldn't believe it if I told you."

I got him my car, opened one of the RC Colas, and opened the Moon Pie. As I pulled out of the small parking lot, I took a bite of the Moon Pie and washed it down with a gulp from the RC Cola. From then on, I was hooked.

As I drove onto the highway and headed back to Little Rock, Patrick's story played over and over in my head. I began to assemble my story for the 50th anniversary of World War I, a little over four months away.

# CHAPTER 32

THE ARTICLE

With only a couple of weeks until my article is released, I called Pauline and asked if I could drop by so they could read it beforehand. Without hesitation, she said yes and asked what I wanted for dinner.

The next day, I drove to Bald Knob. As I drove up to the house, Patrick and Pauline were sitting on the porch. When Sarge saw my car, he sat up. Patrick took off his harness and let him run to me once the car was stopped. I grabbed my briefcase from the passenger seat, got out, and by that time, Sarge was waiting for me with his tail wagging. I pet him and walked up to the porch.

Pauline started to get up, and I said, "Please sit down." I walked over to her, bent down, and hugged her. I then walked over to Patrick and did the same. As I took my seat, I could already smell Pauline's baking from the porch.

I turned to her and asked, "Is that a peach cobbler?"

She smiled and replied, "Yes, with fresh peaches by the way."

Before I could ask, Patrick said, "With strawberry ice cream. I already made it."

All I said was, "Yummy."

We all sat there in silence for a bit, then I said, "Patrick, I have the article, and I want you to read it before it's published." I opened my briefcase and pulled out a Braille version of the article.

"I printed it in Braille so you could read it. Here you go."

He reached out, and I placed it in his hand. I then pulled out two copies and the photograph she gave me. I handed Pauline the picture and a copy of the article.

She looked at the photograph and smiled, clutching it against her chest and mouthed, "Thank you."

I could see that Patrick had already started reading. Pauline took a deep breath and began to read as well.

* * *

**Arkansas' Veterans of World War I**

Fifty years ago, the War to End All Wars was over. By the end of the war, 71,862 Arkansans fought, 2,183 died, and 1,751 were injured. A significant number of the Arkansans were African Americans. I recently had the opportunity to interview a few of Arkansas' heroes.....

* * *

I watched as they both read the article. Patrick's fingers passed over every raised dot. He looked up and said, "I met Eli a few years ago. We met at the VA hospital in Little Rock. He is a good guy. I loved reading what you wrote about him. His time as a prisoner of war is a remarkable story."

He continued to read. I looked at Pauline, and she was wiping away tears from her eyes. I got up and asked, "Are you okay?"

"Yes, yes. The stories are amazing. How brave were these soldiers, in some cases, boys? Some are no older than your son. Her statement hit me right in the heart. My son might have to fight in the Vietnam War, and it was raging with no end in sight.

When Patrick got to his section, he stopped reading and asked, "Gordon, can you read my section, please?"

I replied, "Of course. Pauline, are you okay with that?"

She nodded.

I picked up my copy and began to read.

"Every one of the veterans I interviewed had their own unique story to tell. Patrick King of Bald Knob was no exception. His story begins when he received his draft notice in late spring or early summer 1917. Then he was off to Camp Greene in North Carolina for basic training. Completing basic training, he was assigned to an Infantry squad of the 30th Infantry Regiment, 3rd Infantry Division, in northern France.

However, his story isn't solely about his heroic actions in the war, for which General Pershing awarded him the Distinguished Service Cross. The second-highest award the country can give a soldier. He was awarded the medal for being part of a patrol in enemy territory along the Marne River, mid-July 1918. The information provided by the patrol to General Pershing and his military planners was instrumental in enabling the 3rd Infantry Division, also known as the Rock of the Marne, to repel a much larger German force and turn the tide of the war. Even to this day, they carry that motto.

I met him and his beautiful wife, Pauline, last July. While we sat on their porch, he retold a story about how he was awarded the medal. But it wasn't all about him. It was all about Sergeant Stevens, Scotty, Rusty, Lar, and Willy—the other members of that patrol. The ones that didn't make it home. However impressive his retelling of that fateful day in Northern France was, what he did after the war is what makes Patrick my hero.

Did I mention that Patrick is blind? He was blinded on that same patrol. Not to let his blindness hinder him, when he got home, he set his path on assisting other veterans. By letting them know, there are numerous opportunities available to them despite their injuries. The number of veterans he helped can't be counted, nor can the impact he had on their lives and the lives of their families be measured. He volunteered for up to a couple of years. All the traveling back and forth from Bald Knob to Little Rock took its toll on him.

But those veterans at the VA hospital weren't the only ones he helped. I'm a veteran of World War II, and by listening and talking to him that day, the burden of that war was lifted from my shoulders as well. What I didn't know or expect was that he and Pauline would change my life for the better.

When I first started talking to Patrick, he abruptly got up, went inside, and started playing the piano. Not a happy tune, but one that struck one to their core. I asked Pauline, "He plays the piano?"

She replied, "Yes. That talent was discovered while he was in rehabilitation in England. But the tunes never sounded so dark."

"However, by the time we finished the interview, his playing was one of tranquility, happiness, and calmness. By retelling his experiences, he could finally leave his war behind in France, fifty years later. But it's never too late to heal. He and his wife are truly remarkable people whom I consider my family.

The one thing these interviews taught me is that if you're having any issues, every Soldier, Marine, Airman, Sailor, or Coast Guardsman should reach out to a fellow veteran, family member, a VA representative, clergy, or a caregiver. There is always someone to lean on. The burden is not all yours. When you signed up, you never un-sign up. You sign up for life. Reach out, it's never too late, not even fifty years later."

When I finished, I saw Patrick's head nod in approval. Pauline was crying, not sad tears but happy tears. We all got up and hugged. Even Sarge was in on the hug.

Patrick said, "Gordon, please sit down. I have something to say. Now that I have talked this over with Pauline, it's no surprise to her. When I'm gone, I want you to tell the entire story. Every word I spoke, I left nothing out. I want everyone to know about Sergeant Stevens, Rusty, Lar, Scotty, and Willy. Tell them how I got back. I don't care if some think I'm crazy. I know what happened. Some will see that there is more to life than we know, and that there are guardian angels; I had mine. Will you do that for me, please?"

I sat there for a minute absorbing everything he just said. I looked at Pauline, and she nodded.

I replied, "Yes, I'll do it. What do you want me to title it?"

He took off his glasses, tapped the floor of the porch with his cane, and, with a big smile, said, "How does War on the Porch sound?"

**The End**

# EPILOGUE

## CLOSURE

In the months following my interview with Patrick and Pauline, I would visit every few weeks and have breakfast, of course, along with an RC Cola for lunch (after my article was posted in the paper). I searched for Sergeant Stevens' gravesite. I knew that finding it would provide Patrick with closure.

What I didn't know was whether Sergeant Stevens had been returned to the States at his family's request or buried in the Meuse-Argonne American Cemetery, at Romagne-sous-Montfaucon, France. After conducting some research, I found that from 1919 to 1922, over 44,000 bodies were returned to the United States for burial.

I had two critical pieces of information regarding Sergeant Stevens that would help me locate him: his name and the location where he was killed. With that information, I set out on my quest to find Patrick's hero. My first search was with the American Battle Monuments Commission, established by Congress in 1923. It maintains records of those buried and memorialized at WWI military cemeteries overseas, but not those who were repatriated for burial in the United States. Through the commission, I discovered that

Sergeant Stevens was buried in the Meuse-Argonne American Cemetery in 1921.

So, I decided to contact the cemetery directly after speaking with the superintendent at the Meuse-Argonne American Cemetery. I discovered that there was no grave for Sergeant James W. Stevens.

In addition, the cemetery didn't maintain records of where the bodies had been sent to in the United States. With this information, I was reasonably sure that Sergeant Stevens' family must have requested his body be returned. I felt I was at a dead end, but I had one remaining option for finding Sergeant Stevens. As a reporter, I was fortunate enough to know Senator J. William Fulbright of Arkansas. Although he was not a veteran himself, he strongly supported veterans. I hoped he would provide me with a contact at the National Personnel Records Center (NPRC). Senator Fulbright tasked his aide to assist me in my mission. However, I was also aware that not being a family member might make it difficult to obtain information. The aide contacted the director and shared Patrick's story. The director of the NPRC, a World War I veteran himself, was more than happy to help, and after a couple of weeks, he contacted me with the location of the soldier's burial site.

As the director spoke, I shook my head in disbelief. Sergeant Stevens' grave was only a three-hour drive from Patrick's house, located at the West Tennessee State Veterans Cemetery, situated outside Memphis.

I was overjoyed, but I wondered to myself, had I overstepped my bounds? With the new information, I called Pauline and asked if I could visit the next day, without telling her why. Of course, and said yes.

* * *

I drove up to Patrick and Pauline's house, stopped the car, and got out. Before I was even a few feet from my car, I could hear Sarge starting to bark. Patrick must have taken his harness off, as he ran to me with his tail wagging. Both Patrick and Pauline were sitting on the porch. I had been so busy with the paper that it had been a few months since I had seen them, and Patrick had noticeably aged. He was not as spry as he had been when I interviewed him. He looked frail.

I stepped onto the porch and said, "Hey, Pauline and Patrick, thanks for letting me stop by. I hope you both are doing fine."

They both nodded, but I could see the pain in Pauline's eyes. She knew Patrick was slipping away, and there was nothing she or the doctors could do. She motioned for me to sit down next to Patrick, in the spot I had occupied the previous year. She offered me some sweet iced tea, but I refused. I didn't want her to go into the house to get it. I wanted her with Patrick when I shared the information with him.

I reached out and grabbed Patrick's hand. I noticed he was still wearing his wristwatch. I leaned in and said, in a very calm voice, "Patrick, I know where Sergeant Stevens is buried."

He lifted his head, his lips quivering, and said, "I never asked you to find him. Why?"

I replied, "Patrick, you helped me, and I just wanted to repay you. I'm sorry if I did anything wrong. I can leave now."

I let go of his hand and got up. As I stood, I looked at Pauline, who by now had tears in her eyes. She got up, hugged me, and said, "Gordon, thank you. It's been rough for a couple of months. He is not himself these days."

I smiled, said goodbye, and walked off the porch.

Patrick stood up and yelled, "Hey, Gordon, where? Tell me where."

I stopped abruptly, turned around, returned to the porch, and replied, "Near Memphis at the national cemetery."

Tears were running down his cheeks as he mumbled, "I want to see him. I need to see him. There is something I need to say to him. Please."

"Patrick, the doctor said you couldn't drive long distances," said Pauline.

With a smirk on his face, he replied, "I'm not driving. Gordon is. Right?"

I shrugged and replied, "It's early. We can be there by one and back here by six-thirty or so. It doesn't get dark until around seven anyway. If Pauline agrees, I'm in."

Halfway through my reply, Pauline had already entered the house to grab her handbag and Patrick's medication. She walked out the door, locked it, and said, "Come on, you two."

Pauline hadn't seen Patrick move so fast in months. He reached out to Sarge, put his harness back on, took the reins of his harness, and stepped off the porch.

As we walked to my car, Patrick said, "Hold on, I need to get something out of the house. Pauline, can I have the keys, please?"

He held out his hand, and she pulled the key from her purse and handed it to him. He walked back into the house with Sarge as we waited by the car. It didn't take him long to retrieve what he had gone to get. As he exited the front door, I noticed he put something in the front pocket of his pants.

As he walked toward the car, Patrick put out his hand, the keys dangling from it. Pauline took the keys and held his hand. He stopped and said, "Now, I'm ready, let's go."

I hurried in front of her to open the rear passenger door. She glanced at Patrick and noticed something. He appeared nervous.

We all got into my car. Patrick, Pauline, and, of course, Sarge, were seated in the rear for the drive to the national cemetery.

* * *

After a couple of hours of driving west on Hwy 64 East, I turned south onto Hwy 78 and then east onto I-40. I then took the exit for Hwy 72 west toward Collierville. I looked in the rearview mirror and saw Patrick sleeping. About halfway to Collierville, I noticed the sign for the West Tennessee State Veterans Cemetery. I took the exit and drove to the cemetery. As I was about to pull into the parking lot, I saw that Patrick had woken up.

As he did, he asked, "Where are we?"

I answered, "Pulling into the parking lot of the cemetery."

I stopped the car, looked in the rearview mirror, and said, "Well, we are here."

I got out and opened Pauline's door, then went to the other side and opened Patrick's. Sarge was sitting between them, asleep. As soon as Patrick moved, he woke up and waited for him to get out. I grabbed Patrick's arm and helped him out. Sarge followed him and waited for Patrick to grasp his harness.

"Well, Gordon, let's go." He and Sarge started to walk off.

"Hey, hold on, Patrick. You don't know where he is buried," yelled Pauline.

I replied, "Pauline, I beg to differ. He is walking right to him. He is buried near that big white oak," pointing to the tree in front of them.

Patrick and Sarge stopped to wait for Pauline and me.

Pauline put her arm under his. I led the way as we approached the grave site. I glanced over at Patrick. I saw something in his face that I had never seen, even after learning his story. He moved as if he were on a mission—a mission only he understood.

I said, "Well, here we are," as we stood next to Sergeant Stevens' grave.

Patrick released Sarge's harness and asked, "What is on the headstone?

I stepped closer to the gravestone and read it to Patrick,

"On top of the marker is a cross, James W. Stevens, Sergeant, World War I, 30th Infantry Regiment, 3rd Infantry Division, Tennessee, 11th of July 1918."

As I read it, tears welled up in his eyes.

"Yep, that is him," he said with his voice trembling. Then he asked, "What's on the back?"

I looked at Pauline and shrugged my shoulders. I stepped around the marker and read it to him, "As in front there is a cross, Betty Stevens – May 7th, 1898 – July 2nd, 1918 – Taken too soon. God Rest Her Soul."

"Pauline, help me down, I want to kneel," he asked Pauline.

As he knelt beside his grave, Sarge lay next to him. Pauline and I stepped back. While we stood there, we could hear a faint voice—it was Patrick's. I put my arm around Pauline, and she rested her head on my shoulder without saying a word.

This is what Pauline and I heard: "Sergeant Stevens, I'm here because of you. I still don't understand how or why, after all these years, there is not a day that goes by that I don't think of you. You saved my life and gave me hope that I would be able to return home. Every day that I was in the hospital, I asked the doctors over and over where you were. When General Pershing told me you were dead, my reply was, No, no, he is not. He guided me to safety. He is alive. How else would I have managed to get back? I'm blind. I was hoping they were wrong. I wished all these years they were wrong, but I knew you died in that village on a muddy street in Northern France, on a warm summer night with the soldiers you loved and led into battle. Now I know it was not the physical you. It was your soul that guided me. I hope you are proud of me and the things I've accomplished because of what you've done for me. Thank you. I hope that my presence here brings you closure and that your soul finds peace. It does for me."

Patrick took what he had in his front pocket and laid it on the grave. I asked, "Patrick, what is that?"

While he knelt, he replied, "A letter Sergeant Stevens gave me to hold onto for him. I promised him I would give it back."

Curiosity got the best of me, and I asked, "Did you ever read it, or have it read to you?"

As he stood up, he replied, "No, it's his letter. I can only guess. I think it is a letter informing him that his wife died, I assume from influenza."

He stood at attention and saluted. Turning around, he grabbed Sarge by the harness, walked toward the car, and said, "I'm ready to go home."

Suddenly, he said, "Did you feel that?"

Pauline asked, "Feel what?"

He smiled and replied, "The cool breeze."

I walked over to Pauline, and before I could ask the question, she said, "I had no idea about the letter. He never mentioned it to me. Never."

* * *

When we all got back in the car, Patrick took off his wristwatch, held out his hand, and said, "Gordon, I want you to have this."

I immediately replied, "Patrick, I can't take that, thank you though."

"No, Gordon. I want you to have it. From one warrior to another. Please let this old man release his past."

I looked back at Pauline, and she nodded. I took the watch and put it on. I had received a few medals in the Army Air Forces, but this gift was very special. I got out of the car, walked around to the passenger side, opened the door, and gave him a big hug, then saluted him. As I hugged him, he said, "Now don't forget to wind it every day."

"Yes, of course. Did you already wind it today?" I asked.

He smiled and replied, "Yep, just like clockwork."

I got back into the driver's seat, and we left for the return trip to Bald Knob.

* * *

Taking the same way home, we were almost there, and no one had said a word since we left Sergeant Stevens' grave site. I heard Sarge whine. I glanced in the rearview mirror, and tears were streaming down Pauline's face. I pulled off the highway close to McCory.

I ask her, "Pauline, are you okay? What's wrong?"

I will never forget her response.

She looked at me, then at Patrick, and said, "Take us home, please, Gordon, take us home."

That is when I noticed Patrick was not breathing."

She said, "Some time after Wynne, he peacefully passed away."

Even in death, Pauline protected him, not saying a word, just holding him with her head on his shoulder.

We sat in silence as we were stopped on the shoulder of the highway.

It was eerily quiet when I heard the sound of ticking. I looked around and didn't see anything. I glanced at my wrist and noticed that the watch Patrick had given me was now working. I shook my head, closed my eyes, opened them, and took another look. Sure enough, it was running, and the second hand was moving. At that moment, I thought back to something Patrick said when I interviewed him: "Time stopped, but my life didn't."

I shifted the car into drive and returned to the highway. My mission was to get Pauline and Patrick home. I would not fail.

* * *

Patrick was buried in the National Cemetery at Little Rock, Arkansas. I escorted Pauline and sat next to her. Before lowering his casket into the ground, she was handed the folded United States Flag, which had draped his coffin. A twenty-one-gun salute followed that. In the distance, I could hear a trumpet play taps. Tears started to run down my cheeks.

As I sat there, I felt a calming hand on my shoulder. I turned and said, "Thank you, son."

After the taps, I felt a cool breeze sweep through me. I whispered to Pauline, "Did you feel that?"

She looked at me, smiled, and said, "The cool breeze? Yes, I felt it."

When the ceremony was completed, I looked around. There were mourners as far as the eye could see. They were the veterans whom Patrick helped during his years of volunteering. His family of veterans was together.

I recall asking him once if he knew how many veterans he had helped. Well, seeing all the mourners at his funeral gave me my answer. However, I saw only a small portion, a fraction of the actual number he helped in over forty years of volunteering.

I helped Pauline up as she stood beside me. Smiling, she said, "I will be buried on top of him. Together forever."

The three of us stood there: me, Pauline, and my son, dressed in his Army Class A uniform. He would be shipping off to Vietnam within the month.

Before we walked away, I saluted my hero, "Patrick Wayne King."

# GLOSSARY

**Advanced Dressing Stations (ADS)** - These were located further back from the front line, providing more advanced care, including wound cleaning and preparing soldiers for evacuation.

**Aluminum Identification Disks** – Small aluminum disks with the soldier's name, regiment, and religion. Today, they are commonly referred to as "dog tags." Each soldier carried two. One would remain with the deceased soldier, and the other was taken as proof of death.

**Arkansas Gazette** - A newspaper printed in Little Rock, Arkansas, from 1819 to 1991. It was known as the oldest newspaper west of the Mississippi. In 1991, it published its final edition. Its assets were sold to the owners of the Arkansas Democrat, which was subsequently renamed The Arkansas Democrat-Gazette.

**Artillery Battery** – Four cannons under the command of a captain. The battery was divided into two cannons led by a lieutenant.

**Azimuth** – Refers to compass points from $0°$ to $360°$. $90°$ is east, $180°$ is south, $270°$ west and $360°$ is north. Soldiers used a map and an azimuth to navigate from one point to another.

**Bangalore Torpedoes** – An explosive charge used to clear obstacles. The explosive charge can be a single tube or multiple tubes connected.

**Blitzkrieg** – *"Lightning War,"* a military strategy employed by Germany in the early days of World War II. The strategy combined armor, infantry, artillery, and air assets to overwhelm enemy armies in short, decisive campaigns.

**Bronze Star** - A United States Armed Forces decoration awarded for heroic or meritorious achievement or service in ground combat. It is awarded to service members who distinguish themselves by acts of heroism, outstanding achievement, or meritorious service, not involving aerial flight, while serving in any capacity with the U.S. Armed Forces.

**Browning Automatic Rifle (BAR)** – A family of American-made semi-automatic and automatic rifles. The rate of fire for the BAR was 500 – 650 rounds per minute. It was first introduced in late summer 1918, during World War I. One BAR was assigned per squad.

**Bunker-buster, the 37mm M1916** – Used by U.S. soldiers to destroy German machine gun nests. It was equipped with a telescopic sight for better accuracy.

**Bayonet** – A sharp-edged knife designed to fit on the end of a rifle.

**Casualty Clearing Stations** - These stations provided further assessment and treatment, including minor surgeries and wound care.

**Commanding Officer (CO)** – The leader of a company/battery/troop-sized unit. Usually, a captain. However, in aviation units, the CO might be a major.

**Distinguished Service Cross (DSC)** - The United States Army's second-highest award for valor, second only to the Medal of Honor. It recognizes extraordinary heroism in action against an enemy of the United States. The DSC is awarded for actions that, although not quite reaching the level of valor required for the Medal of Honor, still display exceptional bravery and a significant risk to life.

**Entrenching Tool (E-Tool)** – A small shovel used by soldiers to dig foxholes and carried on their backpacks.

**Evacuation** - Wounded were transported by stretcher-bearers, ambulance trains, or other vehicles to more advanced hospitals, often in cities like Paris or along the coast.

**Flak** - Anti-aircraft shell that bursts in the air.

**Fiddler's Green** – A term used by modern-day cavalry units to memorialize the deceased. Fiddler's Green was a fire support base in the Vietnam Military Region III in 1972, manned by the 2nd Squadron, 11th Armored Cavalry.

**French Chasseurs** – A term referring to hunters, it was applied to light infantry French and Belgian units, as well as light cavalry units. Troops are trained to engage the enemy rapidly.

**French Resistance** – A collective of groups that fought against the Nazi occupation of France during World War II.

**First Sergeant (E8)** – The highest-ranking enlisted soldier in a company, troop, or battery in the U.S. Army. The first sergeant reports to the commanding officer and is responsible for maintaining discipline and overseeing the day-to-day operations of the unit.

**Forward Observer (FO)** – A soldier or soldiers who provide advanced warning of enemy troop activity and movement, then report it back to their unit.

**Friendly Fire** - Weapons fire that injures or kills someone from the same side or an ally in a conflict, rather than the enemy.

**Gewehr 98** – Rifle used by German troops in World War I.

**Grid Coordinates** – Used to locate a specific point or position on a map. The location can be within 1000 meters or as precise as 10 meters.

**German SS** – Schutzstaffel, a paramilitary wing and elite guard organized under Hitler and the Nazi Party.

**German U-boats** – Is a slang name for German submarines.

**Gestapo** – The secret state police of the Nazi party within Germany and its occupied countries.

**High crawl** - a military movement technique where a soldier moves quickly on their hands and knees, keeping their torso off the ground. This allows for faster movement than a low crawl while maintaining a low profile.

**Hospital Blues** - Soldiers who were recovering in hospitals wore a distinctive uniform known as "Hospital Blues." This uniform, also referred to as the "convalescent blues," was designed to be loose-fitting, comfortable, and easily identifiable as belonging to a recovering soldier. It consisted of a blue wool flannel jacket and trousers, a white shirt, and a bright red tie.

**Infection** - The dirty conditions of the battlefield and the limited availability of antibiotics led to a high incidence of infections.

**Kitchen Police (KP)** – Additional duties other than cooking are given to soldiers to assist in the mess hall or dining facilities.

**Line of Departure (LD)** – An imaginary line used for an attacking army to start the attack. Units are required to cross the LD at specific times.

**Livre** – French for a book. Soldiers in WWI kept personal books as a means to release frustration, fears, and their experiences.

**M1 gas mask** – A piece of equipment issued to U.S. soldiers to protect them against chemical attacks (gas).

**M1917 Browning machine** gun – A heavy machine gun used by U.S. forces in World War I, World War II, the Korean War, and the Vietnam War. The M1917 fired a 7.62 NATO round.

**M1911 .45 cal Pistol** – Standard issue sidearm for the U.S. Military from 1911 – 1985.

**MG08/15** – Maschinengewehr 08, the standard German machine gun used in WWI.

**Mausers** – A bolt-action rifle designed by Peter Paul Mauser initially in 1871.

**Mustard Gas** – A human-made sulfur mustard that causes blistering of the skin and mucous membranes upon contact. Large doses were fatal in WWI. It can also cause chronic respiratory disease and permanent blindness.

**Noncommissioned Officer (NCO)** – The backbone of any unit, responsible for maintaining morale and training of the individual soldiers and small unit training. NCO rank is E5–E9. In certain situations, an E4 can be promoted to the rank of corporal and is considered a non-commissioned officer (NCO).

**No man's land** – An area between opposing armies. A term commonly used in World War I.

**Observation Post (OP)** – An area close to the enemy lines that soldiers use to observe and report on enemy activity and movement.

**P-38** – A World War II, single-seat, twin piston-engine fighter built by Lockheed.

**Platoon Leader** – Normally, a 2nd lieutenant leads a platoon and is the officer's first leadership position.

**Prone position** – A firing position where a soldier lies flat on the ground. The most accurate position to fire from.

**Psychological Trauma** - Many soldiers suffered from psychological trauma, such as shellshock, which required specialized care.

**Regimental Aid Posts (RAP)** - This is where wounded soldiers received basic first aid, including stopping bleeding, applying bandages, and providing comfort and support.

**Rehabilitation** - After initial treatment, wounded soldiers often underwent rehabilitation at home front hospitals or convalescent homes to aid in their recovery.

**Salient** – An elongated protrusion of a territory surrounded on three sides.

**Specialized Treatment** - Head wounds, abdominal wounds, and other specific injuries required specialized care, including suture techniques, surgical procedures, and the use of antiseptic solutions.

**Stahlhelm helmet** - The German combat helmet was first introduced in World War I. In service till 1992.

**Stokes mortar** – A smooth-bore metal tube with a metal base plate. Invented by Sir Wilford Stokes and used by the British, U.S., and Portuguese in the latter half of World War I.

**Taps** - The final bugle call of the day on military installations, "Taps" is played at military bases as a signal to service members that it is quiet time or "lights out."

**Trench Knife**—A combat knife used to kill or wound in close combat. It was perfect for trench warfare in World War I. The M1917 was the American version of the knife, featuring a knuckle guard.

**Triage** - The wounded were categorized into three groups: trivial, treatable, and critical. Minor injuries were treated, and the individuals were sent back to the front. Those with more serious but survivable wounds were prepared for evacuation.

**United States Army Air Forces (USAAF)** - The United States Army Air Forces (USAAF) was established on June 20, 1941, marking a significant shift in autonomy from the Army's command structure. This autonomy lasted until 1947, when the Department of the Air Force was established.

**Yperite** – Mustard gas or Sulphur mustard

**1917 Enfields** – Formerly named "United States Rifle." It's a .30 caliber rifle used in World War I.

**1903 Springfields** – A five-round, bolt-action, .30-caliber rifle. It was the standard issue before the introduction of the 1917 Enfield.

**21 Gun Salute** - A military tradition, primarily a naval custom, used as the most prominent form of gun salute to honor individuals and nations. At military funerals, a 21-gun salute is often part of the honors, with the firing of blank rounds by a gun battery.

# BIBLIOGRAPHY


Michael S. Neiberg, *The Second Battle of the Marne*. Indiana University Press, 2008.

Martin Gilbert, *The First World War: A Complete History*. Henry Holt and Company, 1994.

Second Battle of the Marne: https://en.wikipedia.org/wiki/Second_Battle_of_the_Marne

3rd Infantry Division History: https://en.wikipedia.org/wiki/3rd_Infantry_Division_(United_States)

The Art of World War 1 – By Ephraim Durnst. CGR Publishing

World War 1 – The Definitive Visual History – Smithsonian

Uniforms & Equipment of the Central Powers in World War 1 (Volume 1 and 2) – Dr. Spencer Anthony Coil. Schiffer Military History

# ABOUT THE AUTHOR

Travis Davis is an Air Force brat who grew up in Arkansas, Spain, New York, and California. He joined the U.S. Army at 17 years old as an Armored Reconnaissance Specialist and was stationed at various forts in the United States and Germany, where he met his beautiful wife. During his three tours in Germany, he conducted hundreds of border patrols along the East-West German border and the Czecho-slovakia-West German border. He saw firsthand communism and its oppression of its citizens. He retired from the U.S. Army, where his last duty assignment was as Assistant Operations Sergeant of the 2nd Armored Cavalry Regiment at Fort Polk, Louisiana. He is a lifetime member of the Sergeant Morales Club. Travis has also received multiple awards, including the Meritorious Service Medal and five Army Commendation Medals.

# ALSO BY TRAVIS DAVIS

**One of Four: World War One Through The Eyes of an Unknown Soldier**

*• One of Four was selected as the Outstanding "Historical Fiction: 20th Century" Category Winner.*

*• Cover Design and Hemingway Chanticleer Int'l Book Award First Place Win for Fiction Covers and 20th Century Wartime Fiction*

*• FINALIST in the 2024 American Writing Awards!*

*• 2024 International Impact. Book Award Winner*

From New York Harbor to the battlefields of France, relive World War I through the eyes of an unknown soldier, as told through his diary. See how the 100-year-old diary brings a father and his estranged son back together by retracing his experiences fighting in the battlefields of France in 1917 - 1918 to his final resting place—the Tomb of the Unknown Soldier at Arlington National Cemetery.

* * *

**Flames of Deception: Cocked Pistol**

An imagery analyst at the National Geospatial Agency (NGA) analyzing imagery of the oil fields in Western Siberia identifies strange behavior in the oil fields. His keen eye uncovers the best-kept secret in modern history. His intelligence sparked a chain reaction, leading the U.S. government to launch a multi-agency clandestine operation into the matter. At the same time, Russia, China, and India were preparing to conduct the largest naval and ground assault in modern history (codename Bia) to control the transportation of oil through strategic choke points and stop the free flow of oil on land and at sea worldwide. With the help of North Korea, China is planning the most expansive cyber attack on the United States' "Green Energy" power grid. The potential for World War III is real. Can it be stopped?